## Get back in the house!

And the tiny voice inside her, echoing nearly as loud as Grandfather's roar: *Run, run, run!*

Heart thudding, vision blurring, she spun around and dashed away. Dimly, she heard a dog bark, a man shout, but she didn't slow. Her arms swung, her legs were pumping, her strides were closing the distance, but, God, not fast enough.

He caught her, arms wrapping around her, holding her close. His breathing was loud in her ears, his voice unfamiliar as he murmured, "It's okay, Reece, it's okay. Just an old memory. It can't hurt you. They can't hurt you. It's just you and me and Mick. You're safe."

She inhaled sharply, intending to scream, but the scents caught in her nose: soap, shampoo, cologne, dog. She knew those scents. She trusted them.

Jones. Mick.

Pivoting, she wrapped her arms around his neck and held on as if only he could chase away the fear, the ghosts, the memories. Only he could make her feel safe.

She held on for dear life.

\* \* \*

Dear Reader,

I've always liked things that go bump in the night—in theory, at least. I don't like to be scared in real life, though having someone like Jones to hold on to could make the shivers more fun.

Jones is the kind of guy who could make everything better. He's the sort who falls fast and hard; once he gives his trust, it's *given;* and he's kind to crotchety old women and needy puppies. He couldn't possibly be any more perfect for Reece!

Marilyn

# MARILYN PAPPANO

*Copper Lake Secrets*

ROMANTIC
*SUSPENSE*

Recycling programs
for this product may
not exist in your area.

ISBN-13: 978-0-373-27755-1

COPPER LAKE SECRETS

## Books by Marilyn Pappano

---

## MARILYN PAPPANO

has spent most of her life growing into the person she was meant to be, but isn't there yet. She's been blessed by family—her husband, their son, his lovely wife and a grandson who is almost certainly the most beautiful and talented baby in the world—and friends, along with a writing career that's made her one of the luckiest people around. Her passions, besides those already listed, include the pack of wild dogs who make their home in her house, fighting the good fight against the weeds that make up her yard, killing the creepy-crawlies that slither out of those weeds and, of course, anything having to do with books.

To my husband, Robert, who is also kind to crotchety old women and needy puppies. (Even if they do have you wrapped around their pinkies.)

## Chapter 1

*One, two, three, four...*

Counting in her head, Reece Howard moved thirty-eight steps along the ancient brick wall, then counted out another six before reaching the gate recessed into the wall. She counted a lot, but only steps. She'd done it for as long as she could remember—which was only fifteen years with any clarity, a little more than half her life—but who knew why? Maybe she was obsessive-compulsive with that lone manifestation. Maybe she was just freaking nuts. Maybe, her boss suggested—teasingly?—she simply liked numbers.

If that was the case, then she must *really* like the number thirty-eight. That was as high as she went. No more, no less.

It was a warm October afternoon, and Evie Murphy was keeping her regular appointments in the courtyard of her French Quarter home. Evie was many things to

Reece: friend, confidante, counselor, advisor. Officially her title was psychic, and she was very good at what she did, but even her talents had limits.

Evie was waiting at a wrought-iron table and chairs near the fountain. Playing in the grass a few feet away were Jackson, her four-year-old son, and Isabella, her two-year-old daughter. Eight-month-old Evangeline was asleep on a quilt in the nearby shade.

"Aunt Reece!" Jackson flashed her a wicked smile, the very image of his father, and Isabella wandered over, looking around with anticipation. "Puppies?"

"I had to leave the puppies at home today, sweetie. Next time I'll bring them, okay?" Reece slid into the chair across from Evie, who was looking calm and serene and beautiful. Not in the least like the dark, mysterious "Evangelina" who told fortunes for tourists in the shop that fronted the house.

"How are you?"

A lot of people asked the question, Reece reflected, but few put the sincerity and interest in it that Evie did. She was the only one Reece answered honestly. "Terrible. I had the dream again last night. I woke up soaked in sweat with all three dogs staring at me as if I were possessed. And I didn't remember a thing except that it had to do with my time at that place."

She'd used the same words in a recent conversation with her mother, who'd scoffed. *Your time in that place? You spent four months with your grandparents in a beautiful Southern mansion, and you make it sound as if you were incarcerated. Really, Clarice.*

"Your dreams got worse when your grandfather died. Maybe he's sending you a message."

"Like what? I'm next?" Reece retorted. The response startled her, both in its content and vehemence.

Evie's gaze steadied on her face. "Why would you think that?"

Good question. Why *would* she think that Arthur Howard wanted her dead? Besides those months she'd spent in his house, she hardly knew the man. When she tried to picture him, she couldn't bring his face to mind but only images: large, hulking, menacing. And numbers: *one, two, three, four...*

And fear.

"Damned if I know," she replied to Evie's question. "I look at pictures of him, and it's as if I've never seen him before. He's just this blank in my memory." A large, menacing blank.

"You have a lot of blanks in your memory." Evie touched her, her hand warm and grounding. "How many people know what happened that summer, Reece? Three? Maybe four? Your grandfather's death made it one less. If you ever want answers..."

*Go to Fair Winds. Ask your questions.*

They'd had the conversation before, but the idea of returning to Copper Lake, Georgia, to the Howard ancestral home on the Gullah River, tied her stomach into knots. Maybe she didn't really want to know. Her mother was convinced that the best thing she could do was forget the past and move on in the present.

Of course, her mother—Valerie—wasn't the one missing three months of her life, or facing the nightmares, or so full of resentment and distrust that every potential relationship became a burden too cumbersome to manage. Reece was twenty-eight years old, and her only real friends were Evie and Martine Broussard, her boss, and they made it easy for her. They didn't ask for too much; they understood her as much as anyone could.

Much as she loved them, she wanted more. She didn't have grand dreams, but she wanted to fall in love, get married and have children. She would like to make a difference in someone's life, the way her father had made a difference in hers. She would like to be a part of something special, something she'd had in the years before Dad's death had taken it from her: a family.

She wanted, she would like…she *needed*. Answers.

"Ah, Evie, I swore I'd never go back there again."

"You were thirteen."

"I didn't even go back for Grandfather's funeral."

Evie echoed the words Reece had only thought earlier. "You hardly knew the man."

Reece offered her last feeble excuse. "I have to work."

"As if Martine wouldn't let you off at a moment's notice."

Tension knotted in her gut. All these years, her refusal to return to Fair Winds had been a source of anger, frustration and more than a few arguments, but it had been a constant. Valerie had wanted to spend Christmases there; Reece had refused to go. Grandmother had invited them to Mark's wedding; Reece said no. Grandfather had unbent enough to ask her personally to attend Grandmother's seventy-fifth birthday celebration. Reece had stood her ground.

Valerie thought she was childish and melodramatic—ironic insults coming from the woman who embodied both. Grandmother thought she was stubborn and selfish. And Grandfather had told her that her father would be ashamed of her.

*Not as much as he would be of you,* she'd retorted before slamming down the phone. She believed that wholeheartedly. She just didn't know why.

She was tired of not knowing.

Across the table, Evie was waiting patiently. If something bad would come of a trip to Georgia, surely she would sense it. She warned people of danger; she helped them make the right decisions. If she thought Reece should go...

Reece huffed out a sigh. "Okay." Then... "I don't suppose you'd want to go with me."

"And leave Jack alone with the kids? His idea of day care would be sticking them in a holding cell while he interviewed suspects." She squeezed Reece's fingers. "You can call me anytime day or night, and if you need me, I'll come."

A knot formed in Reece's throat, and she had to work to sound casual. "At least you didn't say, 'And take my kids to a haunted house.'"

Her brows drew together. Yes, she had a psychic advisor; yes, she worked in a shop that sold charms, potions and candles to true believers. But ghosts, haunting her father's childhood home? The mere thought should make her laugh, but it didn't. It felt...like truth.

"A place that old, that was worked by slaves, is likely to have a few spirits, but generally they won't harm you."

Maybe. Maybe not. It was impossible for Reece to know what she feared about Fair Winds and her grandparents without knowing what had gone on during those months she lived there.

Grimly accepting, she got to her feet. "All right. I'll go. But if something happens to me while I'm there, Evie, I swear, I'll haunt you for eternity."

Evie stood, too, and hugged her. "I'd enjoy it, sweetie. Now, I'm serious—if you need anything, you call me."

"I will." Though, as she hugged Jackson and Isabella goodbye, she acknowledged she lied. Fair Winds was an evil, forbidding place, and she wouldn't expose these kids' mom to that for anything, not even to save herself.

It was a quick walk from Evie's to the building that housed Martine's shop on the first floor and both her and Martine's apartments on the second. When she walked in, the faint scent of incense drifted on the air, sending a slow creep of calm down her spine. The tourists browsing the T-shirts and souvenirs glanced her way, and she automatically flashed them her best customer-service smile as she passed through to the back room.

"I suppose you're going to ask me to take care of those mutts of yours while you're gone." Martine's back was to Reece as she collected specimens from the bottles and tins that lined the shelves behind the counter. Some customers thought she had a sixth sense, maybe seventh and eighth ones, too, but Reece knew there were mirrors discreetly placed along the tops of the shelves.

"My puppers are not mutts."

Martine sniffed. "What's their breed? Oh, yeah, Canardly. You can 'ardly tell what they are."

"And they love their Auntie Martine so much."

Another sniff before she turned, laying ingredients on the counter. "When are you leaving?"

"What are you, psychic?"

"iPhone and I know all." Martine's wicked grin was accompanied by a nod toward the cell on the counter. "I'll have everything you need in an hour."

*Everything* included charms, amulets, potions and notions. Reece couldn't say from personal experience that they would ward off evil or work to keep her safe, but they sure as hell couldn't hurt. "Then I'll leave in an hour and five minutes."

"You don't waste any time, do you?" Martine asked drily.

The answer was a surprise to Reece, as well, but she knew if she put off her departure for even one day, the dread and anxiety that were tangled in her gut would just keep growing. The drive would give her plenty of time to think of all the reasons this was a bad idea; no use giving herself additional time to wuss out.

"I wish you could go in my place. Grandmother hasn't seen me in fifteen years. She might not notice the difference."

How did Martine make a snort sound so elegant? "Oh, sure, we look so much alike. Maybe the woman's gotten deaf, blind and stupid in addition to old."

Reece grimaced. Though they were about the same height and body type, she was light to Martine's dark: fair-skinned and blond-haired. Having lived all her life in Louisiana, Martine had a pure and honeyed accent, while Reece's frequent moves had left her with a fairly nondescript voice.

"Okay." A sickly sigh. "I'm going to pack and tell the puppers that Auntie Martine will be taking care of them. They'll be so excited."

As she slipped through the rear door and trudged up the stairs, she wished she could dredge up a little excitement.

But all she felt was dread.

Thin streaks of moonlight filtered through the clouds to silver the landscape below, glinting off the stick-straight spears of wrought iron that marched off into the distance on both sides of the broad gate. Spelled in elaborate curls and swoops was the plantation name: Fair Winds.

Though this night there was nothing resembling *fair* about the place. Trees grew thick beyond the fence. Fog hovered low to the ground. No birds sang. No wildlife slipped through the dark. Silence reigned inside the wrought iron.

Jones had been in town for two days and had found plenty of people willing to talk. They said the place was haunted. Strange things happened inside those gates. On a quiet night, wailing and moaning could be heard a mile away.

This was a quiet night, but the only sound drifting on the air came from the dog beside him. Jones laid his hand on Mick's head, scratching behind his upright ears, but it didn't ease the quivering alertness that had settled on the animal the instant he'd jumped from the truck and scented the air.

Mick would rather be in town at the motel or, better yet, back home in Louisville. He liked traveling; he went with Jones on most of his jobs. But he didn't like spirits, and *here, there be ghosties.*

It was his father's voice Jones heard in his head, a voice he hadn't truly heard in fifteen years. His father was loving and generous and good-natured, but he wasn't forgiving. He nursed a grudge better than the meanest of spirits. His two middle sons were dead to him and always would be.

It appeared that Glen really was dead.

Absently Jones rubbed his chest as if that might make the pain go away. He'd been cold inside since he'd heard the news that everything Glen had owned in the world had been found buried under a pile of ancient brush outside Copper Lake. Clothes, books, driver's license, money, photographs, hidden no more than thirty yards from where Jones had last seen him. Maybe Glen would have gone off without his books or his license, even without the clothes or the money, but not without the photos of Siobhan. He'd been crazy mad in love with the girl, had intended to marry her. He never would have left her pictures behind.

And it was partly Jones's fault. All these years, he'd thought Glen was doing the same as him, making a life for himself that had nothing to do with family tradition. All these years, he'd been wrong.

Jones had rushed through his last job when he'd heard the news, then driven straight through from Massachusetts to Georgia. He'd had hours to come up with a plan, but after two days in town, he still didn't have one. All he'd been able to do was think. Remember. Regret.

Had his life been worth everything he'd given up? Doing what he wanted, being what he wanted? If he hadn't gone along with Glen, would his brother still be alive?

Their granny had been big on fate. Things happened as they were meant to, she'd insisted, and he'd been eager to share her belief. After all, that absolved him of responsibility. So he'd broken his mother's heart; it hadn't been selfishness but fate. He'd turned his back on the life his family had embraced for generations because fate had meant him to. He'd denied his heritage and lived for himself because that was the cosmos's plan for him.

But had fate decreed Glen should die before his eighteenth birthday?

Jones didn't think so. Someone else had made that determination, and he wanted to know who.

He figured he already had a pretty good idea of why.

Beside him, Mick gave a low whine. His ears were pricked, his tail stiff, his rough coat bristling. He was staring through the gate at the mists that formed, swirled, then dissipated, only to re-form a few steps away. Ghosts, essence, imprints—whatever you called them, Jones believed in them. His work took him to centuries-old houses all around the country, and every one housed at least one spirit. He didn't bother them, and they returned the favor.

Mick whined again as an insubstantial form separated from the shadows of the live oaks that lined the drive and stepped into the moonlight. Jones's jaw tightened with annoyance. Who would have expected the elderly and recently widowed owner of Fair Winds to be out haunting the place at nearly midnight?

She wrapped fragile fingers around one of the bars on the gate. "Who are you, and what are you doing on my property?"

Mentally kicking himself for coming to the place unprepared, he slid from the tailgate to the ground, felt his wallet shift and immediately knew his approach. As he walked to the gate, he pulled the battered leather from his hip pocket and silently handed her a business card.

It gleamed white as she tilted it to read his name, then tapped it on the bar. "I've heard of you."

He wasn't surprised. The business of historic garden restoration was an insular one. Word of mouth was still the best advertising; a satisfied client was happy to pass on his name to anyone who might be in need of his services. The subject was likely to have come up at least a time or two with the owner of Fair Winds, once home to the most spectacular gardens in the South.

"I've heard of you, too, Mrs. Howard." Then he gestured behind her. "Actually, more of the gardens." It was true. Because of the time he and Glen had spent at Fair Winds, he'd always paid attention when the name had come up. He'd researched the gardens while completing his degree, had seen plans, photographs and praise lavished by guests at the house during the gardens' prime in the 1800s.

"Humph. They haven't existed in the fifty years I've lived here."

"But they're legendary."

"That they are." She tapped the card again. "But that doesn't explain why you're sitting outside my gate close to midnight."

"No, it doesn't." He shrugged. "I'm between jobs, and I found myself in this area. I was curious."

"Curiosity killed the cat, don't you know?"

His smile was cool. "Do I look like a cat to you?"

She stared tight-lipped at him for a moment, then folded her fingers over the card. "Come back tomorrow. You can see more in the daylight." Turning, she took four steps and disappeared into the shadows. The only sound of her passing was the crunch of footsteps on gravel that quickly faded away.

Mick whined again, and after a moment staring into the darkness, Jones faced him. "You're just a big baby, aren't you? Come on. Let's go back to town. We've got work to do."

When he opened the pickup door, the dog jumped into the driver's seat and started to settle in, grumbling when Jones nudged him over the console to the passenger seat. Jones had picked up the shepherd mix at a job in Tennessee. One day he'd appeared at a stop sign, looking into every vehicle that came along before sinking back to the ground. He'd stayed there for days, growing thinner and more despondent, waiting for the owner who'd dumped him to return. Knowing what it was like to be alone and on your own and not sure you were up to the challenge, Jones had begun taking food and water to the stop sign.

On the eighth day, after he'd delivered the meal, Mick had eaten, then walked back to the house with him. They'd been together since.

He followed the hard-packed road to the highway, then turned south. Copper Lake was just a few miles away, but he and Glen had camped on Howard property for a month without going into town once.

Not that it was a bad little town. Once past the poorer neighborhoods on the north side, the town was neat, easy to navigate and excelled at small-town charm. It was home to more than a few magnificent historic houses that made him itch for a sketchpad and pencil.

If he couldn't talk his way into Fair Winds, maybe he could drum up another job as an excuse for staying in the area awhile.

Most of the motels in town were on the lower end, with The Jasmine Bed-and-Breakfast at the high end. He'd picked one in the middle—clean, comfortable, high-speed wireless—and they didn't object to Mick. He parked in front of his end room, let the dog do his business in the narrow strip of grass nearby, then they went inside and he booted up his laptop, calling up the file he'd put together in college and carried with him since.

*Fair Winds Plantation.*

The place where his life had changed. Where his brother's life had ended. Where he intended to find the truth.

A horn blared, long and angry, as a logging truck blasted past, the winds buffeting Reece's small SUV. Dawdling on a two-lane highway wasn't the safest driving she'd ever done, but she couldn't seem to help it. Every time she saw a mileage sign for Copper Lake, her foot just eased off the gas on its own.

Taking a deep breath, she loosened her fingers on the wheel and pushed the gas pedal harder. Once the speedometer reached the posted limit, she set the cruise control. There. The speed was out of her foot's—or subconscious's—control.

She'd spent last night in Atlanta, sleeping badly, tossing through one dark, malevolent dream after another. She was tired, her body hurt, and she had the king of bad headaches. If it were any farther to Copper Lake, she'd be physically ill before she got there.

And yet here she was doing her best to make the trip last.

As the road rounded a curve, a beautiful antebellum mansion appeared on the left, and Reece's fingers tightened again. That was Calloway Plantation. According to the map she'd studied, the turn to Fair Winds was less than a half mile south of Calloway.

Sure enough, there it was, identified with plaques set discreetly into the brick columns on either side. She braked, turned onto the broad dirt road, drove a hundred feet and stopped.

Could she do this?

Evie thought so. Martine did, too. The only one with doubts was Reece herself. Hand trembling, she reached inside her shirt to lift a thin silver chain that Martine had given her. Dangling from it was a copper penny. Appropriate, she thought unsteadily, since she was outside Copper Lake and the taste of both blood and fear, according to people who knew, was coppery.

Evie's calm, confident voice sounded in her head. *If you ever want answers...*

She did. Desperately.

*If you need me, I'll come.*

And Martine: *I'll have everything you need.*

"Except courage." Reece's voice was shaky. "But Grandfather's dead. I'm not thirteen. I can handle this."

She repeated the words in her head as she slowly got the car moving again. Tall pines grew dense on either side of the road, testament to the lucrative logging business that had taken the original Howard's fortune and increased it a hundredfold. As far as she knew, Grandfather had never worked in logging or any other business. He'd managed his investments from his study on the first floor and done whatever caught his fancy. She vaguely remembered fishing poles and rifles and shovels, and the glare every time he'd looked at her...

Before she realized it, she'd reached the gate. It stood open in welcome. She drove through, and the hairs on her nape stood on end. Was it quieter inside the gate than out? Did the sun shine a little less brightly, chase away fewer shadows? If she rolled the windows down, would the air be a little thicker?

"Oh, for God's sake. Valerie's right. I *am* being melodramatic. It's a house." As it came into sight, she amended that. "A big, creepy, spooky house, but still just a house. I haven't entered the first circle of hell."

At least, she prayed she hadn't.

Live oaks lined the drive, huge branches arching

overhead to shade it. The house and its buildings—a guest cottage, the old farm manager's office and a few storage sheds—sat at the rear edge of an expanse of manicured lawn. The brick of the pillars that marched across the front of the house had mellowed to a dusky rose, but there was no fading to the paint on the boards. The colors were crisp white and dark green, but still looked unwelcoming.

A fairly new pickup was parked near the cottage—silver, spotless, too high for a woman of Grandmother's stature to climb into without help. Its tag was from Kentucky, and she wondered as she pulled in beside it if some stranger-to-her relative was visiting. The recent generations of Howards hadn't been eager to stick around Copper Lake. Her father had left at twenty, his brother and most of their cousins soon after.

When she got out of the car, Reece was relieved to note that the sun was just as warm here as it'd been outside the gate and the air was no heavier than anywhere else in the humid South. It smelled fresh like pine and muddy like the Gullah River that ran a hundred feet on the other side of the gate.

She was closing the door when she felt eyes on her. Grandmother? Her housekeeper? The driver of the truck? Or the ghosts her father insisted inhabited Fair Winds?

Ghosts that might have been joined a few months ago by Grandfather's malevolent spirit.

Evie's voice again: *Spirits generally won't harm you.*

Oh, man, she hoped that was true. But if Arthur Howard's ghost lived in that house, she'd be sleeping with one eye open.

The gazes, it turned out, were more corporeal. Seated at a table on the patio fifty feet away, just to the left of the silent fountain, sat a frail, white-haired woman and a much younger, much darker, much... *more*...man, both of them watching her.

Reece stared. Grandmother had gotten *old,* was her first thought, which she immediately scoffed at. Willadene Howard had been frail-looking and white-haired for as long as she could remember, but the frailty part was deceiving. She'd always been strong, stern, unyielding, and in spite of her age—seventy-seven? no, seventy-eight—she certainly still was. She didn't even show any surprise at Reece's appearance out of the fifteen-year-old blue as she rose to her feet. When Reece got close enough that Grandmother didn't have to raise her voice—Howard women never raised their voices—she announced, "You're late."

Maybe she didn't recognize her, Reece thought. Maybe she was expecting someone else. She thought of the responses she could make: *Hello, Grandmother. It's me, Reece, the granddaughter you let Grandfather terrorize.* Or *Nice to see you, Grandmother. You're looking well.* Or *Sorry I missed your birthday party, Grandmother, but I thought of you that day.*

What came out was much simpler. "For what?"

"Your grandfather's funeral was four and a half months ago."

There was nothing Reece could say that wouldn't sound callous, so she said nothing. She walked closer to the table, knowing Grandmother wouldn't expect a hug, and sat on the marble rim of the fountain.

Grandmother turned her attention back to the man, who hadn't shown any reaction so far. "This is my granddaughter, Clarice Howard, who pretends that she sprang full-grown into this world without the bother of parents or family." With a dismissive sniff, she went on.

"Mr. Jones and I are discussing a restoration project we intend to undertake."

Reece's face warmed at the criticism, but she brushed it off as the man leaned forward, his hand extended. "Mr. Jones," she greeted him.

"Just Jones." His voice was deep, his accent Southern with a hint of something else. Black hair a bit too long for her taste framed olive skin and the darkest eyes she'd ever looked into. *Mysterious* was the first descriptor that leaped into her head, followed quickly by more: *handsome. Sexy.* Maybe *dangerous.*

She shook his hand, noting callused skin, long fingers, heat, a kind of lazy strength.

He released her hand and sat back again. She resisted the urge to tuck both hands under her arms and laid them flat on the marble instead. Rather than deal with Grandmother head-on, she directed a question to the general area between them. "The house appears to be in good shape. What are you restoring?" Left to her, she would be tearing the place down, not fixing it up.

"You can't judge a house by its facade. Everything gets creaky after fifteen years." Grandmother's tone remained snippy when she went on. "Mr. Jones is an expert in garden restoration. He's going to bring back Fair Winds' gardens to their former glory. Not that you ever bothered to learn family history, Clarice, but a few generations ago, the gardens here were considered the best in all of the South and the rest of the country, as well. They were designed by one of the greatest landscape architects of the time. They covered fourteen acres and took ten years to complete."

She waited, obviously, for a response from Reece. The only one she gave was inconsequential. "I go by Reece now."

Grandmother's lips pursed and her blue gaze sharpened. Across the table from her, Jones was making a point of gazing off into the distance, looking at neither of them.

"Gardens. Really." Too little too late, judging by Grandmother's expression. The only flowers Reece had ever seen at Fair Winds were the wild jasmine that grew in the woods. Her mother had told her their name and urged her to breathe deeply of their fragrance. Not long after, Valerie had left, the emptiness in Reece's memory had begun and the smell of jasmine always left her melancholy.

A shiver passed over her, like a cloud over the sun, but she ignored it, focusing on the stranger again. Did *just Jones* look like a landscape architect, or whatever his title would be? She'd never met a landscape architect, but she doubted it. He seemed more the outdoors type, the one who'd do the actual work to bring the architect's plans to life. His skin was bronzed, his T-shirt stretched across a broad chest, and his arms were hardmuscled. He was a man far better acquainted with hard work than desk-sitting.

"Sit," Grandmother commanded, pointing to an empty chair as she got to her feet without a hint of creakiness. "Entertain Mr. Jones while I get some papers from your grandfather's study. We'll let him get started, and then we'll talk."

Reece obediently moved to the chair, automatically stiffening her spine, the way Grandmother had nagged her that summer. *Howard women do not slump. Howard women hold their heads high. Howard women—*

The door closed with a click, followed by a chuckle nearby. Her gaze switched to the gardener/architect wearing a look of amusement. "That last bit sounded like a threat, didn't it?"

*And then we'll talk.* It *was* a threat. And even though she'd come there just for that purpose, at the moment, it was the last thing in the world she wanted to do.

Swallowing hard, she tried instead to focus on the rest of Grandmother's words. She might have trust issues and abandonment issues and a tad of melodrama, but she could be polite to a stranger. Her mother required it. Her job required it. Hell, *life* required it. But the question that came out wasn't exactly polite.

"So…is Jones your first name or last?"

# Chapter 2

"Does it matter?" Jones asked, aware his lazy tone gave no hint of the tension thrumming through him. She didn't appear to recognize either him or his name, didn't appear to realize she'd asked him that question once before, the first time they'd met. Had he been so forgettable? Considering that he and Glen had saved her life, he'd think not...but she was, after all, a Howard.

Or was she just damn good at pretending? At lying?

He'd thought he'd lucked out when he returned to the farm this morning to a job offer that would give him virtually unlimited access to the Howard property, but having Clarice Howard show up, too... If there were a casino nearby, he'd head straight there to place all sorts of bets because today he was definitely *hot*.

He'd looked for her on the internet and had found several Clarice Howards, just not the right one. He'd asked the gossipy waitress at the restaurant next to the motel about her, but the woman hadn't recognized the name, didn't know anything about a Howard granddaughter. She'd had nothing but good, though, to say about the grandson, Mark, who lived in Copper Lake.

Mark, who, along with Reece, was the last person Jones had seen with his brother. Mark, who had threatened both Glen and Jones.

"I take it you don't live around here," he remarked.

"No." That seemed all she wanted to say, but after a moment, she went on. "I live in New Orleans."

"The Big Easy."

"Once upon a time." Another moment, then a gesture toward his truck. "You're from Kentucky?"

"I live there." He was *from* a small place in South Carolina, just a few miles across the Georgia state line. He'd been back only once in fifteen years. His father had begun the conversation with "Are you back to stay?" and ended it a few seconds later with a terse "Then you should go." He'd followed up with closing the door in Jones's face.

Big Dan was not a forgiving man.

"What brings you to Georgia?" he asked.

Reece didn't shift uncomfortably in the wrought-iron chair, but he had the impression she wanted to. "A visit to my grandmother."

"She was surprised to see you. You don't come often?"

"It's been a while."

Then her gaze met his. Soft brown eyes. He liked all kinds of women, but brown-eyed blondes were a particular weakness. Not this one, though. Not one who, his gut told him, was somehow involved in Glen's disappearance.

"What made you think Grandmother was surprised?"

"I'm good at reading people." Truth was, he'd heard Miss Willa gasp the instant she'd gotten a good look at Reece. *Lord, she looks like her daddy,* the old woman had murmured. *I never thought...*

She'd ever see her again? The resemblance to her father couldn't have been that surprising. She looked the same as she had fifteen years ago, just older. She still wore her hair short and sleek; she still had that honey-gold skin; she still had an air about her of... fragility, he decided. She was five foot seven, give or take an inch, and slender but not unappealingly so. She didn't *look* like a waif in need of protection, but everything else about Reece Howard said she was.

But appearances, he well knew, were often deceiving.

Deliberately he changed the subject. "Do you know much about the old gardens?"

Despite the change, the stiffness in her shoulders didn't ease a bit. Would she be against the project? Was she envisioning her inheritance being frittered away on flowers and fountains? "No, Grandmother's right. I didn't learn the family history the way a proper Howard should."

History could be overrated. He knew his own family history for generations, but that still didn't make them want any contact with him. They didn't feel any less betrayed; he didn't feel any less rejected.

"I've seen photos from as early as the 1870s," he went on, his gaze settling on the fountain beside them. Built of marble and brick, with a statue in the middle, it was silent, dirty, the water stagnant in the bottom. "They were incredible. Fountains, pools, terraces.

Wildflowers, herb gardens, roses… They covered this entire area—" he waved one hand in a circle "—and extended into the woods for the shade gardens. Fair Winds once had more varieties of azaleas and crape myrtles than any other garden in the country."

"And you're going to replant all that." Her tone was neutral, no resistance but no enthusiasm, either.

"Probably not all, but as much as we can. We have the original plans, photographs, detailed records from the head gardeners. We can make it look very much like it used to."

"What happened to the gardens?"

He shrugged. "Apparently, your grandfather had everything removed. The pools were filled in, the statues taken away, the terraces leveled. Miss Willa didn't say why, and I didn't ask."

Reece muttered something, but all he caught was *mean* and *old.* She'd missed the funeral, Miss Willa had said. Grandfather or not, apparently Reece wasn't missing Arthur Howard.

Shadow fell over them, and the wind swirled with a chill absent a few seconds earlier. A few brown leaves rattled against the base of the fountain, then grew still as the air did.

As Reece did. She sat motionless, goose bumps raised all the way down her arms. He considered offering an explanation—a cloud over the sun, though there were no clouds in the sky; a gust of mechanically-cooled air from an open window or door, though he could see none of those, either—but judging by the look on her face, she didn't need an explanation. She knew better than him the truth behind the odd moment.

Here there really were ghosties.

Did she know what he'd come to find out? Was one of them Glen's?

Before he could say anything else, the door to the house opened and Miss Willa hustled out, her arms filled with ancient brown accordion folders and books. He rose to carry them for her, but she brushed him off and set them on the table. "These are all the records I could lay my hands on at the moment. Clarice may be able to find more in her grandfather's boxes while she's here."

A look of distaste flashed across Reece's face—at the use of her given name or the thought of digging through her grandfather's files?

"Here's the code to the gate—" Miss Willa slapped a piece of paper on top of the stack, then offered a key "—and the key to the cottage."

Surprise replaced distaste in Reece's expression, and witnessing that took Jones a moment longer to hear the words than he should have. Frowning, he looked at Miss Willa. "What cottage?"

"That one." She pointed across the road. "There's no place in town worth staying at for more than a night or two besides The Jasmine, and I certainly don't intend to subsidize The Jasmine when you can stay here and keep your attention on your work."

He generally liked staying at or near the job site. On long-term jobs, he often moved into a small trailer, which beat a motel any day. But he didn't particularly appreciate being told where he would stay, or the assumption that he needed to be told to stay focused on his job. He was a responsible man, and while Miss Willa might well be accustomed to giving orders, he wasn't accustomed to following them, except in the narrow scope of the job.

But he wasn't stupid enough to argue, not when her high-handedness fit right in with his needs.

"I appreciate the invitation." His sarcasm sailed right past Miss Willa's ears, but earned a faint smile from Reece. "I should warn you, my dog travels with me."

"Keep him quiet, keep him away from my house and clean up after him, and we'll be fine." Miss Willa shifted her gaze then to Reece. "Lois is fixing dinner. We'll talk when that's over." With a nod for emphasis, she returned to the house.

The action surprised Jones. Miss Willa hadn't seen her only granddaughter in years, and yet she casually dismissed her?

But wasn't that what his own father had done with him? Hell, Big Dan hadn't just dismissed him; he'd sent him away. Though Jones had betrayed Big Dan. Did Miss Willa think the same of Reece? And was there more to it than Reece missing the old man's funeral?

Reece *wasn't* surprised. Idly she opened one of the books on the table, an oversize title with musty yellow pages and decades-old plates of the most impressive gardens of the post–Civil War South. Jones had a copy in his office back in Louisville. "Grandmother doesn't like to discuss unpleasant matters at the dinner table," she said by way of explanation.

"What could be unpleasant about her granddaughter coming for a visit?"

"A long-neglected visit. I haven't been here since…" Her attention shifted from the book to the house, her gaze taking in the three stories of whiteboard siding and dark green trim, the windows staring back like so many unblinking eyes. "Since I was thirteen," she finished, the words of little more substance than a sigh.

The summer he and Glen had been there. Why?

What had happened to keep her away all that time? A falling-out between her mother and grandparents? A petty argument that had grown to fill the years?

Or something more?

With a slight tremble in her fingers, she closed the book and smiled, but it lacked depth. "Fair Winds isn't my favorite place in the world. It's…"

He let a heartbeat pass for effect. Another. Then he softly supplied the word. "Haunted?"

She startled. Her gaze jerked to him and her arms folded across her middle as if to contain the shiver rippling through her. "You believe in ghosts, Mr. Jones?"

"I told you, it's just Jones. No *Mister.* Why wouldn't a house like this have ghosts? It's nearly two hundred years old. Dozens of people have lived and celebrated and suffered and died here. Some of those spirits are bound to remain."

"You've encountered such spirits before?"

"I have, and lived to tell the tale."

He grinned, but the gesture didn't relax her at all. Instead, a brooding darkness settled around her. "Wait until you've met Grandfather, if he's still here. He might change that."

Jones tucked the security code into his hip pocket, picked up the books and papers, then twirled the lone key on its ring around his finger. "He can't scare me too much," he said mildly as he started across the patio to the road. "After all, he *is* dead."

Dead, but not forgotten, and still possessing the ability to frighten.

At least, he could still frighten Reece.

She watched until Jones had disappeared inside the cottage, wishing she could have claimed it for herself before Grandmother offered it to him. It was a miniature replica of the house, with a huge difference: it was memory-free and nightmare-free. Reserved for visitors, it had been off-limits to her and Mark that summer. At the moment it seemed the only safe place on all of Fair Winds.

But Jones had it, so she was going to be stuck in the house where Grandfather had lived.

And expected to go through his boxes, too. A shudder tightened her muscles as she recalled the one time she'd gone into his study. Only in the house a few days, she'd still been learning her way around, and Mark had told her that heavy dark door that was always closed led into a sunroom filled with beautiful flowers.

There'd been nothing sunny or beautiful about the room. Dark drapes pulled shut, dark paneling, the thick, heavy smell of cigars and age, and Grandfather, glowering at her as if she'd committed an unpardonable sin. He'd yelled at her to get out, and she'd scurried away, slamming the door, to find Mark laughing at the bottom of the stairs. Grandmother had chastened her, and Valerie had, too, and she'd felt so lost and lonely and wanted her dad more than ever.

Oh, God, she wasn't sure she could do this, not even to find out what had happened those three months. Over the course of her lifetime, they added up to what? One percent of her time on this earth? Nothing. Inconsequential.

Except the months did have consequences: the nightmares, the fear, the distrust.

She breathed deeply. Across the drive, Jones came out of the cottage, climbed into his truck and drove away. She felt his leaving all the way to her bones. Aside from Lois, who must be Grandmother's current housekeeper, there was no one left on the property but her and Grandmother.

Not a thought to inspire confidence in a drama princess.

Another deep breath got her across the patio and into the door. Dimness replaced bright sun; coolness replaced heat. Instead of pine, the lemon tang of wood polish drifted on the air, along with the aroma of baking pastry. A voice humming an old gospel tune came from the kitchen, ahead and to the right. Lois, Reece was sure. She'd never heard Grandmother hum or sing, had rarely seen her smile and couldn't recall ever hearing her laugh.

No wonder Daddy had left the first chance he got.

She ventured farther along the hallway that bisected the house north to south. A glance through the first set of double doors showed the table in the formal dining room, set for two. Opposite was Grandmother's study, a small room with airy lace curtains, a white marble fireplace and delicate-appearing furniture that looked hardly a year of its century-plus age.

The rooms were small, the ceilings high, the furnishings mostly unchanged. A broad hallway, easily as wide as the rooms themselves, cut through in the middle from east to west. The stairs rose from this hall, and portraits of early Howards—and, in one case, an early Howard's prized horse—lined the walls. None of Grandfather, Reece noted with relief. His memory was enough to haunt her. She didn't need portraits, too.

The salon was empty, the door to Grandfather's office closed. Presumably Grandmother was upstairs. Readying a room for her? Gathering items Jones might need in the cottage? Or getting ready for the noon meal? After all, Howard women dressed for meals.

Reece paused outside the study door. The house was oppressive. So many rules, so little laughter. Her father had loved to laugh. Elliott Howard hadn't taken anything too seriously. He must have felt so stifled within these walls.

She was about to go upstairs, left hand on the banister, right foot on the first tread, when a creak came from the study behind her. Another followed it, then more: the slow, steady sounds eerily similar to a person pacing. Her fingers tightened around the railing until her knuckles turned white, but she couldn't bring herself to let go, to turn around and walk across the faded Persian rug to the door.

It was probably Grandmother, looking for more papers for Jones, having thought better of the idea of trusting the search to *her.* If she'd wanted company, she would have left the door open; she would have—

"Well, don't just stand there. Either come up or get out of the way."

So much for the theory of Grandmother. The old woman was standing on the stair landing, hair brushed, makeup freshened, a string of pearls added to the diamonds she always wore.

Reece glanced over her shoulder at the study door. The room was silent now. Just her imagination running wild. It always had, according to Grandmother. *That girl lives in a fantasy world,* she'd often complained to Valerie. *Thinks she sees ghosts everywhere.*

Heard them. Reece had never seen a ghost. She'd simply heard them, and felt them.

She loosened her grip on the banister and backed away as Grandmother descended the stairs.

"Dinner is served promptly at 12:30. Supper is at 6:30. If you miss the meal, you fend for yourself—and clean up after yourself." With an arch look, Grandmother passed her and headed for the dining room.

Reece followed her and took a seat at the polished mahogany table as a woman about her mother's age began serving the meal. There was iced tea in crystal goblets that predated the War, salad and rolls served on delicate plates her great-great-and-so-on grandfather had brought from France when he was still a sea captain in the early 1800s, roasted chicken and vegetables, and pie. Much more than the po'boy or muffuletta she usually had for lunch back home.

The conversation was sporadic, nothing more interesting than general comments about the weather or the food. It was ridiculous, really, to chitchat about nothing when they hadn't seen each other in so long, but Reece was no more eager to have a serious conversation than Grandmother was willing to break her dinnertime rules.

It would have been nice, though, to have been greeted with a little more pleasure—a hug, a kiss, an *I'm happy to see you.* Valerie didn't have much patience with her, but even she managed that much every time they met.

Finally, the meal was over and Grandmother, taking her tea along, led the way into her study. It was the brightest, airiest room in the house, but it was stifling in its own way. The furniture was uncomfortable, and Grandmother didn't relax her rules there. A settee that didn't invite sitting, spine properly straight, chin up, ankles crossed and Grandmother with her own rigid posture didn't invite confidences or intimacy.

Grandmother had apparently exhausted her store of chitchat and went straight to the point. "All these years, all those invitations you turned down or ignored, and suddenly you show up without so much as a call. What changed your mind?"

She could claim tender feelings, but Grandmother wouldn't believe her. Reece had always tried to love her; weren't grandmothers supposed to be important in a girl's life? But loving someone who constantly criticized and lectured and admonished... Fearing Grandfather had been easy. Feeling anything for Grandmother hadn't.

Reece gave a simple, truthful answer. "Curiosity."

"Curiosity killed the cat."

How many times had she heard that? And Mark, always out of the adults' earshot, creeping up beside her, his mouth near her ear. *Meow.*

"You look well," Reece said evenly.

"I am well. Your grandfather, however, is dead. Your mother came for his service. Your aunt Lorna came, and Mark and his family were there. Several hundred people were there, in fact, but not his one and only granddaughter."

The desire to squirm rippled through Reece, but she controlled it. Howard women met every situation with poise and confidence. "I couldn't come."

"You mean you wouldn't."

"It's not as if we were close."

"And whose fault is that?"

*His. He never said a nice word to me. He yelled at me. He scared me. He threatened—*

Reece stiffened. Threatened? She didn't recall Grandfather ever actually threatening her, not with tattling or spanking or anything. Was that part of what she couldn't remember? Part of *why* she couldn't remember?

"It was my fault," Reece said. She would take all the

blame Grandmother could dish out if it helped her get a few answers. "That summer I lived here, I was frightened of him. He wasn't exactly warm and cuddly."

To her surprise, Grandmother nodded. "No, he wasn't. But he was a good man."

Maybe in the overall scheme of things. Reece couldn't deny that Mark had adored him. Maybe Grandfather hadn't known how to relate to girls. Maybe he'd never forgiven his older son for leaving and transferred that resentment to her. Maybe asking him to deal with his son's death and a grieving thirteen-year-old girl at the same time was too much. She did look an awful lot like her father.

"That summer," she hesitantly began.

"What about it?"

*What happened? Why do I still have nightmares? Why can't I remember?* The questions seemed so reasonable to her, but she'd lived with them for fifteen years. Would they sound half so reasonable to Grandmother, who hadn't been much better at dealing with a grieving thirteen-year-old than her husband?

"I've been thinking a lot about that summer lately," Reece said, watching Grandmother closely for any reaction.

She showed none. "It was a difficult time for everyone. Losing your father that way... Your uncle Cecil passed four years ago. A mother's not supposed to outlive both her children."

The last words were heavy, as if she felt every one of her seventy-eight years, and sparked both sympathy and regret in Reece. She couldn't imagine losing a child...or having a loving grandmother. If things had been different, if Daddy hadn't moved to Colorado, if Reece had had a chance to know both her grandparents before Daddy's death, would that summer have had such an impact on her?

But Daddy had had issues of his own with Grandfather, so their visits had been few. They'd been practically strangers when she and Valerie had come to stay.

And there was no wishing for a new past. It was done, and all that was left was living with the consequences.

"I'm sorry about Cecil," Reece said, meaning it even though she hadn't met the man more than twice that she could recall.

Grandmother's unusual sentimentality evaporated. "He ate too much, drank too much and considered riding around a golf course in a cart exercise. It was no great shock that his heart gave out on him. His doctor had been warning him for years about his blood pressure and cholesterol, but he wouldn't listen. He thought he would live forever." Her sharp gaze fixed on Reece. "How long are you planning to stay?"

"I don't know. A few days." No longer than she had to. "If that's all right with you," she added belatedly.

"Of course it's all right. Fair Winds has always been known for its hospitality. I already told your cousin Mark that you're here, so he'll be by to say hello."

Reece swallowed hard. "He lives around here?" That was one thing she hadn't considered. Much as she wanted answers, she wasn't sure she wanted to face her childhood enemy to get them.

"In town. He moved here after college. He and Macy—she's from a good Charleston family—they have one daughter and another on the way. He runs the family business and checks in on me every day."

Reece smiled weakly. "Wonderful."

*Grandfather's dead. I'm not thirteen. I can handle this.*

If she repeated it often enough, maybe she would start to believe it.

Jones stopped at the grocery store to get the five major food groups—milk, cereal, bread, eggs and chips—before going to the motel to pick up his clothes and Mick. When he let himself into the room, the dog was stretched out on the bed, the pillow under his head, the blanket snuggled around him. He lifted his head, stretched, then rolled onto his back for a scratch, and Jones obliged him, grumbling all the time.

"You are the laziest animal I've ever seen. You eat and sleep all day, then snore all night. You've got it made."

Mick just looked at him, supreme satisfaction in his big brown eyes.

"We'll be bunking in a new place for a while. There will be room for you to run as long as you stay out of Miss Willa's way. She doesn't strike me as a dog-friendly person." Jones considered it a moment. "She's not a particularly people-friendly person, either. But we've dealt with worse."

And there was the consolation prize of her granddaughter, whose own eyes were as brown as Mick's but way less happy and a damn sight less trusting. He didn't think it was just him, either. She didn't seem the type to warm up to anyone quickly, if at all.

That was okay. Pretty as she was, all Jones wanted from her was information. She was still a Howard, still a part of Glen's disappearance, and he was still the kid who'd been taught wariness and distrust of country people—anyone outside of his people, regardless of where they lived—from birth.

But she was awfully pretty, and she did have that vulnerable-damsel thing going on that neither he nor Glen had ever been able to resist.

But he would resist now.

After loading his bags and Mick into the truck, Jones slid behind the wheel and left the motel, turning west on Carolina Avenue. Catching a red light at the first intersection, he drummed his fingers on the steering wheel until, beside him, Mick whined. Jones glanced at the dog, an admonishment on his tongue, then forgot it as his gaze settled on a man in the parking lot twenty-five feet away.

He was about Jones's age, an inch or two taller, maybe thirty pounds heavier, and he wore a light gray suit so obviously well made that even Mick would recognize its quality. He was talking to a young woman, a briefcase in one hand, keys in the other, and he stood next to a Jaguar. He was fifteen years older, a whole lot softer and a hell of a lot better dressed, but Jones would have recognized him anywhere.

A horn sounded, and Jones's gaze flicked to the traffic light, now green, then back at Mark Howard. The sound drew his attention, and he looked at Jones, their gazes connecting for an instant before Howard dismissed him and turned back to his conversation.

Hands tight on the wheel, Jones eased the gas pedal down, resisting the urge to turn the corner, pull into the lot, grab Howard by the lapels of his custom-tailored suit and demand the truth about Glen. There would be a time and a place to talk to the man, but this was neither.

By the time he'd turned north on River Road, a bit of the tension had seeped out. He liked Copper Lake. It was the quintessential small Southern town, war memorials in the square and the parks, beautifully restored antebellum homes. The people were friendly and happy to answer questions. No one had treated him with suspicion...though so far he hadn't asked any questions that sounded suspicious. He hadn't brought up the subject of Glen's disappearance or the discovery of his belongings or his gut instinct that the Howard family was responsible. If he started asking that sort of question, they were likely to close ranks and protect their own.

Mick sat straighter in the seat when Jones turned off the highway onto Howard property. Shutting off the AC, Jones rolled the windows down, and the mutt immediately stuck his head out to sniff the air. When they drove through the gate, though, Mick drew it back in, let out a long, low whine and moved to the floorboard to curl up.

"Baby," Jones accused, but Mick just laid his head on his paws. The dog knew the place was unsettled. Reece knew it. How the hell could Miss Willa not know, or if she did, how could she continue to live there?

The road continued past the cottage, leading to the other buildings. Jones drove past the small house, then pulled onto ground covered with a heavy layer of pine needles. The spot would block the view of his truck from any casual visitors to the house—maybe not a bad thing once Miss Willa's grandson and others found out she was planning to spend a ton of money on their grand project.

"Come on, buddy, let's get settled." Jones climbed out and stood back, but Mick didn't stir. "Mick. Out."

The dog gave a great sigh, but didn't move.

"C'mon, Mick, out of the truck now." He stared at the dog, and the dog stared back.

He'd never had a battle of wills with an animal that

he hadn't won, and today wasn't going to be the first. He snapped his fingers, an unspoken command that Mick always responded to, but the mutt just whined once and hunkered in lower.

"I guess we know who's the boss in this family."

Jones started. He'd been so intent on the dog that he hadn't even heard the crunch of footsteps on the gravel, and apparently neither had Mick. He reacted now, though, stepping onto the seat, sniffing the air that brought a faint hint of perfume and smiling, damn it, as he jumped from the truck and landed at Reece's feet.

She offered her hand for Mick to sniff, then crouched in front of him, scratching between his ears. "You're a big boy, aren't you? And a pretty one. I don't blame you for wanting to stay in the truck. I don't much like this place, either. But we do what we gotta do, don't we, sweetie?"

Jones watched her slender fingers work around Mick's ears, rubbing just the way the dog liked. Hell, Jones liked a pretty woman rubbing *him* the same way, and Reece certainly was pretty crouched there, her khaki shorts hugging her butt, her white shirt shifting as her muscles did. For the first time since she'd climbed out of her car a few hours ago, she looked almost relaxed, and he doubted he'd ever seen her look that trusting.

Did she ever offer that much trust to a human being? To a man?

"He's usually not that stubborn," Jones remarked, leaning against the truck while Mick offered a toothy smile. It was almost as if the mutt was gloating: *I've got her attention and you don't.*

"Animals are sensitive."

"You have dogs?"

"Three. All throwaways. Like me." The last two words must have slipped out, because her gaze darted to him, guarded and a bit anxious, and a flush colored her cheeks. He knew from Glen that she'd had abandonment issues that summer. Her father hadn't chosen to die in that accident, but the end result was the same: he was gone. And her mother had preferred Europe with her friends over taking care of her daughter.

Jones could sort of relate, except from the other side of the matter: he was the one who'd done the abandoning. Had it cost Reece's mother as much as it had him? Did she share even a fraction of his regret?

"Mick was dumped near a job site. When he got tired of waiting for his owners to come back, he decided to live with me."

"Lucky you. After I fed the first stray outside the store where I work, he brought two more with him the next day. They've been living with me ever since."

"Too bad you couldn't bring them with you." Traveling with dogs could be a hassle, but their company was worth it.

"Dogs in Grandmother's house? And not even purebreds?" She scoffed as she stood.

Reaching into the bed of the truck, he took out his suitcase and laptop, then started for the porch. To his surprise, the rustle of plastic told him she'd taken out the grocery sacks and was following.

Mick jumped onto the low porch while Jones and Reece went to the steps in the center. He propped open the screen door, unlocked the door, then stood back so she and the dog could enter first.

The door opened directly into the living room, with the kitchen a few feet to the right. To maximize space, there was no hallway, just a door off the living room that went into a bedroom. He guessed the bathroom could only be reached from that room.

"I always wanted to see this place." Reece set the grocery bags on the kitchen counter and automatically began unpacking them.

He laid his own bags against the wall. "You lived here and never came inside?"

The refrigerator, a recent model, closed with a thud after she put the milk and eggs inside. "Did I say I lived here?"

The undercurrent of wariness to her voice stirred its own undercurrents in Jones. He, who'd always been cautious of what he said to country people, never should have made such a stupid slip. "I just assumed you grew up around here."

She considered the words a moment as she crumpled the plastic grocery bags together, then shrugged. "I stayed here for a few months when I was thirteen. My cousin Mark was here, too, that summer. This cottage was off-limits to us. Grandmother said it was for guests, not hooligans who ran wild."

He forced a grin. "Hooligans? She actually called you hooligans?"

Her own smile was half-formed. "She did. Grandmother had—has—very exacting standards that we often failed to meet."

Jones didn't know about Mark, but apparently Reece was still something of a failure in Miss Willa's opinion. The old woman certainly didn't approve of Reece's long absence or missing her grandfather's funeral. That was the sort of thing that got a person disinherited by a prideful woman like Willadene Howard.

Was that why Reece had come now, because her grandfather was dead and her grandmother was nearing eighty? Did she want to get back in Miss Willa's good graces before she passed and left everything to cousin Mark?

Or maybe she'd heard about Glen's stuff being found. Maybe she wanted to make sure there was no suspicion, no effort to find out what happened to the boy who'd saved her life and, apparently, lost his own as a consequence.

Jones watched her wander through the living room, giving Mick on the sofa an affectionate pat as she passed, and hoped neither suspicion proved to be true. Maybe she had come to realize over the years that family was important. Maybe she regretted not making peace with old Arthur before his death and didn't want similar regrets when Miss Willa was gone.

God knew Jones had regrets about his family. He liked his life. He loved his job. But if he could do it all over again, he couldn't say he would make the same choices. There was a lot he hated about his family's way of life, but…he'd missed so much. He hadn't gotten to stand up at his brothers' and sisters' weddings. He had nieces and nephews he'd never met. Birthdays and holidays and anniversaries, celebrations and funerals, good times and bad…

Reece broke the silence. "The furniture looks like it's been here since the cottage was built."

"It probably has. There's a fortune in Chinese antiques in this room alone." He opened the drapes, letting in the afternoon light, before sitting on an unpadded imperial rector's chair. "The Howard who originally settled here was a sea captain. There's a maritime phrase, *Fair winds and following seas.* A wish for good weather. That's where the name comes from."

Head tilted to one side, she sat beside Mick, resting

her hand on his back. "I didn't know that. I told you, I didn't learn the family history."

"He acquired treasures from all over the world. I'm sure Miss Willa's given you the rundown of some things in the house."

"Some. I was always terrified, using lamps and dishes and furniture that were irreplaceable. Being afraid made me feel clumsy and insignificant."

There it was again—that hurt. Vulnerability. She'd grown up. She'd gone from cute and awkward to beautiful, from a child to a capable woman, but it didn't seem as if time had done a thing to change that part of her.

*Seem.* Which meant it wasn't automatically true. She could be a world-class manipulator. After all, she still hadn't acknowledged that they'd met before. She hadn't asked the obvious question: *How is your brother?* After all, she'd spent a lot more time with Glen that summer than with Jones.

Leaning back in the chair, he rested his ankle on the other knee. "Those months you stayed here…this must have been a great place to run wild. All the woods, the creek, the river…you and Mark must have had some fun times."

"Not particularly."

"You didn't get along?"

A jerky shrug. "He was a fourteen-year-old boy. I was his thirteen-year-old girl cousin. I think we were genetically predisposed to not get along."

"So what did a thirteen-year-old girl do for fun out here alone?"

Her expression shifted, darkness seeping into her eyes, caution into her voice. "I read a lot. Spent as much time away from the house as I could."

The reading part was true; she'd been lying in a

patch of sunlight near the creek reading the first time he and Glen had seen her, and she'd always brought books along every other time.

"Didn't you have someone to play with? A neighbor's kids?"

The caution intensified before she answered on a soft exhalation. "No."

Realizing he was holding his own breath, Jones forced it out and did his best to ignore the disappointment inside him. Okay. So she was a liar. It wasn't a surprise. It wasn't even a real disappointment. She was a Howard, and Howards were part of that segment of rich, powerful people who felt money raised them above everyone else. They weren't bound by the rules that applied to everyone else. They were, as Miss Willa made clear at every turn, *better*.

Truthfully, though…he *was* disappointed.

# *Chapter 3*

"So...did you and Miss Willa have that talk?"

Reece studied the contented expression on Mick's furry face, feeling homesick not for her apartment, but for her dogs. It sounded trite, but they loved her in ways no human ever had, besides her dad, and he'd left her.

"We did. It was all warm and fuzzy." She grimaced to let him know she was grossly exaggerating, then quickly changed the subject. "Where do you start on this project?"

"Studying the history. Walking the property. Making sketches. Figuring a budget." He paused before asking, "Do you think it's a waste?"

"The place could only look better with gardens." The beauty of the gardens would offset the ugly creepiness of the house...maybe. Or the creepiness of the house might turn the gardens brown and lifeless, like itself.

"I mean the money."

Reece gave a little snort, a habit she'd picked up from her dad that neither Valerie nor Grandmother had been able to chastise out of her. "It's her money. Why should I care?"

"Because when she passes, presumably it becomes your money. At least, part of it."

The concept of family meant a lot to Grandmother, but she drew the line at rewarding the weak, the flawed or the obstinate. Reece had never given it any thought because she'd just assumed Mark and his mother—the good Howards—would inherit the bulk of the estate. She doubted there was any heirloom indestructible or worthless enough for Grandmother to entrust it to her.

"She took care of us after my father died, and she paid for my college." Two years at Ole Miss before Reece had gone to New Orleans for a weekend and never left. "She's done her duty to us."

"Do you think your cousin will feel the same?"

The muscles in her neck tightened. "I don't have any idea how Mark will feel. I don't know him."

"But you said he was here the summer you were."

"And I avoided him as much as possible."

"You haven't seen him since? Talked to him?"

She shook her head, though, of course, that would soon change. No doubt, he would be here before too long, for both his daily visit and to scope out the reason for *her* visit.

"Not real close to your family, are you?" Jones asked wryly.

"I see my mother two or three times a year. I talk to her once a month. That's close enough." Again, she turned the conversation to him. "I suppose you come from one big, happy family. Every Sunday when you're home in Louisville, you all get together after church for dinner, mint juleps and a game of touch football in the backyard, and you talk to your mama every day like a good Southern boy."

She expected acknowledgment, or a chuckle. Instead, shadows passed over his face, and his mouth thinned. "It would have been South Carolina, after Mass for barbecue and beer, then watching a game on TV. But no, we're not close. I haven't seen them in a long time."

Discomfort flushed her face. She wouldn't have said anything if she'd known that their two replies together would cast uneasiness and regret over the room as surely as a thunderhead blanketed the sun. At the moment, this room felt no more secure than the big house.

Except for Mick, snoring beside her. Abruptly he came awake, ears pricking, a ruff of skin rising at the base of his neck. He jumped to the floor and padded to the screen door, where a low growl rumbled in his throat.

At the sound of a vehicle approaching, Reece's gut tightened. Moving with much less grace, she joined the dog at the door, grateful for the deep overhang of the porch roof that granted some measure of camouflage.

The car coming slowly up the drive—no need to let speed throw up a chunk of gravel to ding the spotless metal—looked expensive, though if it weren't for the sleek cat captured in midpounce as a hood ornament, she couldn't have identified it. But Howards—all of them except her and her dad—liked luxury in their vehicles. Valerie switched between a Mercedes and a Cadillac every two years. She wouldn't even ride in Reece's hard-used SUV.

Without making a sound, Jones came to stand behind

her, not touching but close enough that the heat radiating from his body warmed her back and the scent of his cologne replaced the mustiness of the cottage in her nostrils.

Together they watched, Mick trembling with alertness beside them, as the Jag parked next to her truck. Reece's breath caught on the lump in her throat when the door opened and the driver appeared in the bright sunshine.

*Curiosity killed the cat.*

*Meow.*

She might not have seen him in fifteen years, but she had no doubt it was Mark. He'd gotten taller, carried too much weight in his midsection and his hair was thinning, but he still possessed the ability to make her hair stand on end, to raise goose bumps down her arms and to make her stomach hurt.

"Want to go say hello?" Jones murmured.

Both she and Mick looked back at him only briefly before focusing on Mark again. The dog growled, a quiet, bristly sound, and she felt like doing the same thing.

But she had no choice. She would have to face him sooner or later. Besides, he was a grown man now. He'd probably changed. And he well might have some of the answers she was looking for.

Drawing a deep breath, she laid one hand on the screen door.

"Want company?"

Going out there with Jones at her side—better yet, in front of her—sounded so lovely and *safe.* But he would probably have to face his own run-in with Mark once her cousin found out about the garden project.

"Thanks, but…I'd better…"

It took another deep breath to get her out the door and down the steps. She'd reached the drive before something made Mark turn in her direction. He stopped near the fountain, just looking at her as she approached, then slowly a smile spread across his face and he extended his hand, moving the last few feet to meet her. "Clarice! God, it's been a long time."

The instant his fingers closed around hers, he pulled her into a close embrace. Panic rose in her chest, but she controlled it, holding herself stiff. After just a moment, he released her, stepped back and gave her a thousand-watt smile. "You're no longer that skinny little kid I used to torment. Of course, I'm no longer that snotty little brat who liked to torment. Grandmother must be ecstatic about having you here."

*Not so you'd notice.*

Nor did he notice that she didn't answer. "Grandmother's kept me up on you. Living in New Orleans, still enjoying the single life. I'm married, you know. We were sorry you couldn't come to the wedding, but Valerie told us how busy you were. We have one kid, Clara, and another on the way." He pulled out his cell phone in a practiced manner and called up a photo of a brown-haired chubby-cheeked girl. She was about eighteen months, sweet and looked far too innocent to carry her father's blood.

"She's a doll." Reece's voice was husky, her tone stiff.

"Yeah, she's my sweetheart. Next one's going to be a boy, though. Just think of the fun I'm going to have with him." He returned the phone to his pocket, then settled his gaze on her again, his features settling into seriousness in an instant. "I made life pretty awful for you, didn't I? I'm sorry about that. I was a dumb kid, and I was so jealous of you being here. It was *my* summer visit, too, and I wanted Grandfather and Grandmother all to myself. I behaved with all the maturity of…well, a dumb kid. It's a wonder you didn't beat the crap out of me back then."

Something passed through his blue eyes with the words. Chagrin? Regret? Or something a little more… hostile?

Reece was sorry she couldn't be unbiased enough to tell.

Then he shrugged, a careless gesture she remembered well. As a kid, he had literally shrugged off everything—her pleas, Grandmother's requests, Valerie's infrequent attempts to admonish him. The only person he'd never tried it with was Grandfather. They'd been two of a kind, the old man had laughed.

"Let's go in and find Grandmother," Mark suggested, taking her arm. "I try to check on her every day. She's not as young as she thinks she is. Macy and I have asked her to consider moving into town—we have a guest cottage at our place that we built just for her—but you know how stubborn she is. She's convinced that she can do everything she did thirty years ago, but we worry about her out here alone."

Half wishing she could pull away and make a wild dash for her truck, Reece let herself be drawn across the patio to the door. Everything inside was just as it had been when she'd left a half hour ago: cool, dim, quiet, oppressive. Maybe a little more so than before…or was that her imagination?

Grandmother was at her desk in the salon, spine straight, fountain pen in hand. Reece hadn't seen a computer in the house, and no doubt Grandmother would disapprove of any correspondence that didn't include Mont Blanc and her favorite ecru shade of engraved Crane & Co. stationery. She'd been raised in a different era, and with the kind of money both her family and the Howards had, she could get away with remaining firmly rooted in the customs of that era.

When they entered the room, she finished her note, put the pen down and lifted her cheek for Mark's kiss. The affection between them—as far as any affection with Grandmother went—was easy, almost natural.

Mark claimed he'd been jealous of Reece. For a moment, she was jealous of him. She would have liked having a normal relationship with a normal grandmother who didn't constantly find her lacking.

"So you two have got your greetings over with," Grandmother stated as she moved from the desk to the settee with Mark's gentlemanly assistance. "And did you meet Mr. Jones while you were out there?"

"Mr. Jones?" Looking puzzled, Mark settled in beside her while Reece chose a spindly-legged chair opposite. "Is he traveling with you, Clarice?"

"I guess she didn't tell you she answers to Reece now." Grandmother's quiet little huff was all she needed to say on that subject. "No, Mr. Jones is a landscape architect whose specialty is restoring old gardens."

Mark stopped short of rolling his eyes. "That again, Grandmother? I've never seen anyone so fascinated by gardens she never laid eyes on. They're gone. Dug up. Grown over. You can't bring them back."

"*I* can't, obviously, but Mr. Jones can. He has quite an admirable reputation in this field."

Mark's eyes started another roll but stopped again. "Grandfather had those gardens removed for a reason, Grandmother. It was important to him. Have you forgotten that? Are you actually considering disregarding his very clear feelings on the matter?"

Grandmother gazed out the window for a moment as if lost in time, then replied with every bit of the stubbornness Mark had mentioned earlier. "Yes, I believe I am. Not just considering it, in fact, but doing it. Mr. Jones started work today."

Reece watched Mark closely: the faint fading of color from his cheeks, the thinning of his lips, the distress that settled over his face. "You've signed a contract with him? You've committed to this—this insanity? Grandmother—"

Her arch look silenced him. "Of course I haven't signed a contract with him." But just as relief sagged Mark's shoulders, Grandmother went on. "Robbie hasn't had time to draw it up yet. First Mr. Jones has to present me with plans and costs, and that will take some time. It's an enormous job, putting back everything Arthur undid. It will take a great deal of time and, yes—" her sharp, accusing gaze moved from Mark to Reece, then back again "—a great deal of money. But it's my money, at least until I die, and I'll spend it as I please."

Reece resisted the urge to raise both hands to ward off the warning. She didn't want the old woman's money. Sure, a windfall would be nice. Having the cash to get a place of her own where the dogs could run free—and where she could take in more homeless dogs—would be fantastic. But she earned enough to live on and to support a few luxuries—Bubba, Louie and Eddie—and she'd never expected anything more.

Mark, clearly, expected more.

"Grandmother, you can't be serious. Do you have

any idea how big those gardens were? How much they cost?"

"Yes, I do. As someone who's been *fascinated* by them since I came to live here, I know quite a lot about them, and so does Mr. Jones. Restoring Fair Winds will be a major coup for him. He'll have more business than he can handle after this."

Reece suspected he already had plenty of business. A man didn't get…how had Grandmother put it? *Quite an admirable reputation* without some major clients. No matter whose gardens he'd worked on, Grandmother would, of course, consider hers the most important.

"But, Grandmother—"

She interrupted him, something she considered rude and common—a sign of how determined she was to see this plan through. "Have you forgotten, Mark, that I'm in charge of my own affairs? When I want advice, I'll ask for it, and I'll ask an expert, not you. At this moment, I'm not asking. I'm simply informing you of my plans. Don't worry. There will be money left over for you and Macy and the children. You'll have your inheritance, but I will have my gardens."

Moving far more spryly than most women her age, Grandmother rose from the settee and left the room.

The silence was heavy, and just a bit darker as clouds blocked the sun and the windows fell into shadow. Uneasiness creeping up her spine, Reece wanted to make her exit, too—right out the door and onto the patio— but something kept her in her seat.

"Oh, my God." Mark dragged his fingers through his hair, the gesture drawing attention to how much it had thinned in fifteen years. Another five, and he'd likely be completely bald on top, as his father had been. As her father might have been if he'd lived long enough.

Forever couldn't have been long enough to suit her.

"Did you know about this?" Mark asked suddenly. "Is that why you just showed up after fifteen years without so much as a call?"

There, faint in his voice, in his eyes, was the hostility she remembered. Along with the shadows, it lowered the temperature in the room a few degrees.

"No. Jones was here when I arrived. They had pretty much completed their discussion by then."

"Sorry." Actually sounding it, he ran his hand through his hair again. "I can't believe... I thought I had talked her out of... We can't let her do this. I'll talk to Robbie Calloway—he's her lawyer—and see what we can do to stop her. Do you have any idea how *much* this will cost?"

"It won't be cheap." Martine shared the tiny courtyard of her building with Reece and the dogs, barely big enough for a fountain, two chairs and all the plants they could cram in, with a few patches of grass for the four-legged residents. Lush and lovely as it was, she doubted it would cost more than $100 to replant the entire thing.

"Wow, you have a way with understatement." Mark gave her a rueful smile. "We're talking tens of thousands, hell, probably hundreds of thousands of dollars. For some stupid flowers and bushes. What in hell is she thinking?"

Reece made her voice mild. "I imagine she's thinking that it's her money and she should spend it on what makes her happy."

The flash of friendliness disappeared under the weight of a scowl. "Maybe you're happy living in an apartment in the French Quarter, but that's a few hundred grand that I'd rather have in my kids' college fund than in the dirt out here."

Then his gaze turned distant. "Though she does comment on how beautiful the flowers are every time she comes to the house. Macy has a real green thumb. She planted the whole area around the guest house just for Grandmother."

How many young men would include separate living quarters at their houses for the day an elderly relative could no longer live on her own? How many young wives would embrace the idea? If someone told her *she* had to take in Grandmother or even Valerie to live, she'd pack up the dogs and disappear lightning-quick.

"You think she should go ahead with this foolishness."

Reece nodded. "I do."

"But she might not even live to—to see it done."

"She knows that." Though Willadene Howard had never answered to anyone on earth besides her husband; she might not answer to death, either, when it came calling.

"So I can't count on you to help change her mind."

"It's not my place. I haven't been here in fifteen years. I can't just show up and start telling her how to spend her money."

"I guess not." He stood, leaned across and tugged her hair. "I've got to get back to town. See you tomorrow."

"I'll be here." Unless Grandmother or the ghosts or the fear she'd lived with so long ran her off.

Out in the hall, he paused long enough to shout, "I'm going, Grandmother. I'll be back tomorrow."

A moment later, Reece saw him through the window, striding to the car as if he'd had nothing but the most pleasant of visits. She was turning back when a flash of movement at the door caught her attention. "Grandmother?"

The only answer was the soft whisper of footsteps on the wood.

"Lois?"

A breeze stirred the curtains, blowing one strip of filmy lace hard enough that it caught on her shoulder before drifting down again and, almost lost on that unseen wind, came a long feline whisper of sound. *Meow.*

Shivers racing through her, Reece stood and hurried to the door. *One, two, three, four, five...*

On summer jobs, where the temperature could be unbearable by noon, Jones usually tried to get a really early start on the job site by the time it was light enough to see. When excessive heat wasn't a problem, he took his time, actually sitting down to eat his breakfast, checking his email, catching up on the news.

That was what occupied him Tuesday morning when Mick trotted to the open door and snuffled. His tail was wagging in a broad enough swath to take down any antiques within range—the reason Jones had spent a good part of yesterday afternoon moving all breakables to a safer place.

After he'd stood at the door the entire time Mark Howard was inside the house. When Mark had come out, he'd looked satisfied, as if he didn't have a care in the world. Had the meeting with Reece gone that well, or was he just really good at hiding his emotions?

Even after Mark had left, Jones had stood there, watching, but Reece hadn't come out again. Neither had Miss Willa.

Now, though, it looked as if he'd have a chance to find out how the reunion had gone, because Mick wasn't wagging his tail so eagerly for the old woman who didn't care for dogs.

Shutting his laptop, he went to the door, unlatching the screen. Mick shot out, barking and bounding down the driveway toward the barn. Sure enough, Reece was a few hundred yards down the road, wearing the short pants his secretary called capris and a bright orange top, her stride long but easy, as if she didn't have a particular destination in mind.

Upon hearing Mick's approach—something similar to a freight train—she turned, then braced herself for any excited leaping. Jones grinned. No jumping was the first lesson he'd taught the dog. He'd guess her own dogs hadn't learned it as well.

Mick immediately sat down in front of her, and she bent to scratch him. Her mouth was moving, but Jones couldn't hear the words until he got closer.

"...such a good boy. You're so pretty, and look at that face. Who wouldn't love such a handsome face?" Her tone was softer than usual, gooier than usual. She was a sucker for four-legged guys, even if the two-legged ones made her a little wary.

"You're gonna spoil my dog rotten," he said from a few yards away.

Her gaze lifted, and wariness did enter it, just a bit. "He deserves to be spoiled. He's a good boy."

"You headed someplace in particular?"

She shook her head.

"Mind if I join you?" At her hesitation, he went on. "I told you yesterday, one of the things I need to do is walk the property. We need to know what conditions we'll be working with, if there are better ways in or out, where we can stage equipment when we're not using it, that sort of thing. Maybe you can show me around."

She was quiet for a time. She glanced at the old barn ahead, then past it where the road trailed off. Regretting that he'd ruined her plans for a quiet morning walk? Or was there something more to her walk this morning? Was she planning to revisit old haunts? Maybe to check that things out there hadn't been disturbed?

Things like Glen's grave?

She shrugged. "I'm not sure how much showing around I can do, but you're welcome to come along. I really don't remember much about the place."

"I thought you said you spent as much time away from the house as you could."

"I did, but it was a long time ago. I was a kid. I didn't pay much attention." She started walking again, and he fell into step with her. Mick raced on ahead, regularly looping back to encourage them onward.

Curious why she was lying about something as simple as knowing her way around the woods, Jones continued subtly probing. "I understand that a creek runs through here somewhere before it empties into the river, and that there's a pool deep enough to swim in."

"Really." She spared him a glance before shifting her gaze down again. The road had petered out and the ground was getting rougher. "I don't like to swim. I can't remember the last time I was in the water."

Jones's muscles tightened. Now *that* was a flat-out lie. He couldn't even count the number of times she and Glen had met at the pool to swim, and she'd done it like a fish. And how the hell could anyone forget the time they went swimming and their cousin tried to drown them?

"You're kidding." He hoped his voice sounded more

natural to her than it did to him. "Everyone likes to swim. What's better on a hot summer day than jumping into the water?"

Her smile was small and unsteady. "Anything, for me. I don't like the water. I'd rather swelter."

Her tone was just short of fervent, but her expression: eyes narrowed, teeth clenched, muscle twitching in her jaw... Was she doing a poor job of lying, or telling the truth with large parts left out?

He couldn't say. He wasn't an expert at detecting liars. If he was, he wouldn't have fallen for the stories of one customer and the beautiful blonde he'd dated a few years back. In their own way, both of them had cost him quite a chunk. Was Reece lying to him? If so, she sure lacked the finesse of the customer and Elena.

As they walked deeper into the pines, he asked, "How did it go with your cousin yesterday? Was he happy to see you?"

"He seemed to be. He apologized for being such a brat."

Was that what the oh-so-superior Howards called attempted murder: being a brat? He'd hate to see how they truly defined a crime.

"I'm kind of surprised he didn't go to meet you when he left the house. Grandmother told him about her plans."

"And he wasn't happy." Jones laughed. "You'd be surprised how often the extended family *isn't* happy. It's a lot of money, and a lot of families would rather see that money in their pockets rather than mine."

"He plans to change her mind. But good luck with that. I think Grandmother is constitutionally incapable of changing her opinion. She doesn't waffle, never sits on the fence and never backs down once she's reached a decision."

"Sounds like my dad. Big Dan has standards, and anyone who fails to meet them is out of his life."

Reece looked at him, her gaze both curious and sympathetic. He realized he'd said more than he meant to, but he didn't try to explain away the words. He was grateful, though, that she didn't ask questions. *What standards did you fail to meet? Is that why you're not close? Did you disappoint him?*

Standards regular people would applaud him for turning away from.

But his people weren't regular people. If they were, he'd probably still be there in South Carolina, living close to the family, a part of their everyday lives.

To fill the lull, he gestured around them. "Did you know your family used to be in the logging business? That's why these trees are planted in rows."

"I did know that." She sounded relieved for the mundane subject. "How do you know about Fair Winds?"

"I visited here once a long time ago, when I was a kid." He watched her peripherally, but no reaction crossed her face. "When I went to college, I came across some articles on it, remembered it and began collecting information."

"You must have been excited when Grandmother contacted you about redoing the gardens. What a coincidence, huh?"

"Not at all. I contacted her. I was in the area, my crew doesn't need me at our other job sites, and I wanted to see the place again. When I told her what I do, she offered me a job."

"It's that easy to get such a large contract?"

"Not usually. Must have been fate." Like Granny always said.

A shape took form in the woods ahead to the right, shadowy, its sharp, straight, man-made lines softened by the vines that grew over and around it. With a touch on Reece's arm, Jones steered her in that direction and onto the faint remnants of a rarely used trail.

Wrought iron encircled the Howard family cemetery, its paint faded and peeling where it poked free of the vines. Two brick pillars marked the gate, with another in each of the four corners. In the center stood a marble bench, and rows of markers marched away from it in all four directions. The rusted gate was propped open, and he walked through it, getting to the third row of headstones before realizing that Reece still stood at the gate, looking distinctly uncomfortable. Mick sat beside her, apparently understanding this was a place he shouldn't go.

"Ghosts rarely haunt cemeteries," he said quietly. "They attach to places or people that were important in their lives, not their deaths."

She moved forward enough to lean against the brick. "Do your clients know you believe in ghosts?"

"Unless the place has its own ghosts, it usually doesn't come up." He gazed over the oldest markers: 1821, 1845, eight from the Civil War. Most were elaborately carved: name, spouse, sometimes children, date of birth, date of death, a bit of poetry or Scripture. One had a carving of a galloping horse, another a sculpture of a fallen tree. The infants' graves bore hearts or angels.

"Is that Grandfather's grave?"

He didn't have to hear the quaver in Reece's voice to know she was uneasy, didn't have to see her gesture to locate the newest grave toward the back of the plot. The earth was no longer bare. Grass had grown over, and a tendril of vine from the nearest fence was beginning a slow curl around the base of the stone.

"It is. Arthur Belvedere Howard." He was reading the marker, massive, granite—a hard stone for a hard man—when Reece slowly came to stand beside him. She stared at the grave as if she feared the old man might reach up through the ground and yank her in.

"When my mother told me he had died, all I could feel was relief." She spoke so softly that Jones could barely hear her despite the quiet around them. "I hardly knew the man. I don't remember much about him. But I just thought, 'Oh, good. He's gone.' Valerie—my mother—pitched a fit when I told her I wasn't coming for the funeral. She kept saying, 'He was your *grandfather*,' as if that meant something, but when my only response to his passing is, 'Oh, good,' how much can it possibly mean?"

Jones studied her—the sheen of sweat on her forehead, the moisture glistening in her eyes, the faint quiver of her lower lip, the insubstantial voice, as if she was afraid to say out loud the things she'd just murmured—and his gut tightened. Was it possible... Had the old man...

They were ugly words: abused. Molested. Hurt. He didn't want to think them. But it would explain her feelings toward her grandfather. It would account for her avoidance of family and this place for fifteen years.

It could also explain her insistence that she didn't know her way around Fair Winds, her not recognizing him and her denial that she'd had contact with anyone else that summer. A kid whose father had just died, whose mother abandoned her, whose cousin tormented her and whose grandfather molested her... Any one of those could be reason enough to block that time from her mind.

He turned away from the headstone, revulsion making him queasy.

"What made you decide to come back now?" he asked as he started back toward the gate.

She caught up with him at the brick pillars, and they set off into the woods again, following the path of least resistance. "Truthfully?"

"Call me strange, but I always prefer the truth." In an effort to lighten the gloom from the cemetery—and chase those ugly thoughts from his mind—he wryly added, "Except about Mick. Don't tell me my dog is homely or has bad breath."

"He's a beautiful boy, and his breath smells just like doggy breath should." She swiped away the sweat on her forehead, then detoured around a fallen pine. "My psychic—who also happens to be one of my best friends—suggested it."

She walked on a few feet before looking at him. "No laughter? No horror? No 'Uh-oh, she's crazy'?"

"I told you, I believe in ghosts. Why should I think going to a psychic is crazy?" Besides, he had generations of female relatives who'd made decent money in fortune-telling. Most of them had been frauds, but there had been a few true seers in the bunch. His granny had been one of them.

"Evie's legit. I know they all claim they are, but she really is. And she's a good friend, too. She knows I have some...issues, and she thought coming here would be good for me."

Jones heard her words, but right after "issues," he stopped paying attention. They'd reached the easternmost side of the farm, marked by a wooden fence that had long ago been painted white, gleaming even out here in the woods out of everyone's sight. He recognized the small hollow between the trees, the not-too-distant trickle of water from the creek, the lone crooked pine that grew at a forty-five-degree angle over the fence.

This was where he and Glen had camped during their time at Fair Winds.

This was the last place he'd seen his brother.

# *Chapter 4*

Reece felt as if she'd intruded someplace she wasn't wanted. It wasn't a new feeling, by any means, just unexpected. Jones had been so friendly from the start; she hadn't expected him to suddenly forget she was there.

She looked around, wondering if it was something about the place that had yanked his attention away, but there was nothing remarkable about it: a small clearing surrounded by trees. The creek ran nearby, and they were close enough to the highway to hear passing traffic. Other than that, it was woods, like the rest of the property.

She stayed where she was while he walked into the open area, then slowly turned. For a moment, he stared off to the northeast, and she had the strangest sensation that he'd left her. Sure, his body was there, but *he* wasn't. She was alone.

Just as slowly, he completed the circle, then looked

at the ground, the bent tree, cocked his head and listened to something—the creek? The breeze? A ghost?

After intense scrutiny, his exhalation was loud enough to startle her. He realized that she was watching him, but he didn't try to brush off the odd moment. "This place..." he murmured.

"Is haunted."

His smile was thin, almost...sad. "Yeah."

They didn't talk much after that. They tramped through the woods, Mick staying close most of the time, running off on occasion to trail some forest creature. Reece tried to open herself to the place, searching deep inside for a familiar memory. She didn't find it, not in the trees, the trails, the creek or the pool where it widened to an idyllic swimming hole.

Jones suggested they stop there, and they sat at opposite ends of a crude bench, one long slab of wood hammered atop two shorter ones. It looked old enough to have been built by the very first Howard, but she guessed it was probably Mark's work when he was younger. He'd liked swimming, fishing, hunting—those guy things he shared with Grandfather—while she'd had nothing in common with the man but blood.

The thought made said blood run a little cold.

"You mentioned your other job sites," she said at last. "How many jobs do you have going at once?"

"No more than one major one, usually, like this, but we've got a lot of smaller jobs. Enough to keep me busy and on the road most of the time."

"You like being on the road?"

He grinned. "It's in my blood. My father and grandfathers have spent a large part of their lives on the road."

"And your mother and grandmothers?"

"Wait at home."

"Nice, I guess. If you don't want to actually spend time with the man you're married to." It wouldn't work for her. She'd been looking a long time for Mr. Right. Once she found him, she'd like to share her bed with him more often than not.

"They spent enough time together. Both my grandmothers had seven kids, and Mom and Dad had six." Leaning forward, he scooped up a pinecone, broke off a chunk and tossed it into the water, where the current danced it out of the pool. "You ever come here before?"

"Not that I recall. I told you, I don't swim."

"Yeah, but what kid can resist throwing things in the water?" He tossed another small piece, then a second. As they bobbed along, an old memory came to mind: her and her dad at the duck pond in Denver. How many hours had they spent on a concrete bench not much better than this one, tossing in stale crackers and chunks of bread for the ducks and talking about the wonders of life? Of course, to a nine-year-old, everything was pretty wondrous.

The wish that it still was ached deep in her chest.

"This one," she answered in response to his question.

With a grin, he shook his head. "You must have read an entire library's worth of books that summer."

Maybe. In dire need of escape to a world where things still made sense, she'd read a lot those first weeks, when she wasn't crying and trying to convince herself it was all a horrible nightmare and she would wake up soon. After that…

Well, that was why she was here. To find out.

For the hundredth time, she wondered if knowing was really important. It didn't take a psychiatrist to know that there was a *reason* she'd blocked that summer out. Something bad had happened that her thirteen-year-old mind had deemed unbearable. Was she any better equipped to deal with emotional trauma at twenty-eight?

Evie thought so. Martine did, too. Sometimes so did Reece. But sometimes…

She was about to suggest they get moving again when a wind blew over them. Elsewhere around them, the air remained still; the leaves didn't rustle; the branches didn't sway. The current was icy and bore hints of smells: sweat, brackish water, fresh dirt, rain, tobacco. Goose bumps raised on her arms, and she hugged herself tightly to contain a violent shudder.

When she managed a look at Jones, he was watching her. The skin on his arms was pebbled, too, but he wasn't shivering. He sat as still as stone.

As quickly as it had stirred, the wind stopped. For an endless moment, the woods were silent as a morgue, until one brave bird chirped. Another swooped from one tree to the next, and the usual chatter slowly resumed.

Jones stood, his movements smooth and easy, and extended his hand. She wasn't sure she could have stood without his help. Her legs were unsteady, her hands trembly and her insides awhirl.

They'd gone a hundred feet, her hand still clasped inside his big, warm one, before he spoke. "Now that's something you don't experience every day."

She laughed, just a little, enough to ease some of the tension making her vibrate. "I think it's safe to say that most people don't experience ghosts every day." As relief and calm seeped into her, self-consciousness flooded her, and she eased her hand from his and put a few more feet between them. "My father used to tell me stories about this place. Grandmother said they were all nonsense, and Grandfather...well, he thought pretty much everything about Daddy was nonsense. They didn't get along. The first time I can remember coming here for a visit, I must have been five or six. As soon as we walked into the house, I started asking, 'Where are the ghosts, Daddy?'" She shook her head. "My grandparents were not amused."

"Did you see anything?"

"I never actually see them. I hear things. Feel things. Footsteps, that wind, creaking, emotions." She looked up. "Do you see anything?"

"Sometimes just wisps or vague shapes. But usually not."

The conversation might have struck anyone else as ridiculous, but not Reece. Besides her own sensitivity to other presences, Evie talked to spirits and they talked back, and Martine had her own experiences with things otherworldly. It was a common thing in their small circle.

"But Miss Willa doesn't believe."

"Oh, no. So if you have any trouble with the ghosts when you start digging up the yard, don't expect her to understand."

"I'll keep that in mind."

The trees thinned ahead, allowing the sunlight through, and the house became visible. Jones's gaze fixed on it. "It's a beauty, isn't it?"

Reece tried to appreciate the house from a purely architectural view. The symmetry of windows and doors was nice. The porch that stretched across the front was shady and cool in the morning, sunny and warm in the afternoon. It was a wonderful place for watching storms sweep across the river. The bright white and the crisp green paint contrasted starkly with each other, and the faded brick softened the whole effect.

It was exactly how a plantation-era house should look.

But where Jones saw beauty, she saw despair. In every one of those windows reaching three stories high, she saw unhappiness. Gloom. Unsettledness. Cold. It was the most unwelcoming place she'd ever been and, having grown up with Valerie, that said a lot.

"I'm afraid I'm too biased to answer that fairly."

A slight figure rose from one of the rockers on the porch and faced their direction. Grandmother. It was too early for lunch, so probably a good time to talk to her. Reece had tried a couple of times the afternoon and night before, but it was just so hard to start the conversation.

Her experience with Valerie didn't make it any easier. Every time the word *summer* came from Reece's mouth, even if it was something as innocuous as a mention of summer vacation, her mother tensed, lines appeared at the corners of her mouth and a look passed through her eyes. *Here we go again.*

But Reece hadn't tried three dozen times to get any information from Grandmother.

"Mick and I are going back to the cottage to get to work," Jones said, his path angling toward the back of the house.

"Coward," she murmured.

"I heard that."

Her own steps slowed until she was barely moving. Once she realized it, she gave herself a mental shake and picked up the pace. As she walked across acres of neatly mown grass, she wondered what had possessed Grandfather to tear up the gardens that had been such a large part of Fair Winds' legend. Surely he hadn't resented the staff needed to care for them. And it couldn't have been a financial decision; he'd had more money than God.

What problem had flowers and shrubs and fountains caused that led him to destroy them?

Long before she was ready, she reached the house. Grandmother had seated herself again, a book open on her lap. Dressed as formally as ever, she slid her gaze over Reece's shirt, capris and sneakers, and her nose crinkled in the slightest *humph,* though she said nothing about Reece's appearance.

She gestured to the nearest chair, green wicker with a floral-patterned cushion. "Have you been getting Mr. Jones acquainted with the property, Clarice?"

"Getting both of us acquainted with it." Reece didn't correct the names. That Jones preferred no *Mister* preceding his name and she generally answered only to Reece was of no consequence to Grandmother. *She* was the arbiter of what was correct and it wasn't open to discussion.

"You spent enough hours out there in those woods. I don't see how you could possibly have forgotten any part of it. Of course, that was a long time ago."

It was as good an opening as any Reece was likely to get. Shifting enough to make the wicker creak, she tried to project a casual attitude, in both voice and posture, as she said, "There's a lot I don't remember about that summer."

"There wasn't much to remember. You got up in the morning, played outside until mealtime and you went to bed at night. Once a week you went to town with me to shop, and on Sunday mornings we went to church."

"All of us?" It was hard to imagine Grandfather putting on a suit, going to church and being sociable.

"You, Mark and I. Your grandfather believed in God. He just thought he was more likely to find Him out there—" she gestured toward the property "—than in some stuffy church."

More likely he'd been afraid that God might strike him down if he stepped through the doorway of the sanctuary.

"So nothing memorable happened that summer."

Grandmother gave her a chastising look. "Obviously not, or you would have remembered it." Gripping the book with both hands, she lifted it from her lap. "I've brought this for you. It's a history of the Howard family. Your great-grandfather commissioned it shortly before he passed. You should know from where—and from whom—you come."

With reluctance Reece took the book. It was heavy, bound in leather, its pages yellowed and its fragrance musty. She couldn't imagine much more boring than a family history where the family chose which facts to include and which to leave forgotten. No doubt every Howard in the book appeared as highly intelligent, benevolent, compassionate, heroic and generous, and from her limited experience, she knew better.

"I'll look at it this afternoon." Not a lie. She would look at it. She just might not open the cover. Though knowing Grandmother, there would probably be a quiz later.

"Did Mark and I get along that summer?"

Grandmother's gaze was directed westward, toward the river barely visible through the live oaks. "Of

course you did. You were cousins. He might have been
something of a pest, but you were rather spoiled and
had a tendency to cry."

*Of course I did! My dad had died and Valerie had
left me here where I hated it!*

"We'd hoped you would grow out of it, and you did
stop tattling fairly quickly, but you were still prickly.
Comes from being an only child, I suppose."

Mark was an only child, as well—and a brat. He'd
gotten her in trouble, blamed her for his own actions
and scared her more times than she could count. But
he'd been the grandchild they knew, the one they could
handle.

The silence had gone on awhile when abruptly
Grandmother spoke again. "I blamed your mother, you
know."

"For spoiling me?" Wrong person. Valerie had been
okay as a mother, but it was Dad who had indulged
Reece. He'd been like a kid himself, finding wonder in
everything they did. He'd loved being silly and making
her giggle, and he'd usually found a way to give her
things Valerie had said no to, without upsetting Valerie, either. He'd had a knack for getting his way without upsetting people.

Which made his estrangement from his parents seem
that much odder.

"For your father's death," Grandmother answered.
"If she hadn't come to Georgia for college…if she
hadn't insisted on going back to Colorado…if Elliott
had been here where he belonged, he wouldn't have
been on the highway that day. He wouldn't have been
hit by that speeding truck." Her voice softened to a
whisper. "He wouldn't have died."

Pain stirred in Reece's chest. One thing she did remember from that time was the *if* game. *If I'm a good girl, Daddy will come back. If I do everything I'm supposed to do, they'll tell me it was a mistake. If I pray hard enough tonight, when I wake up in the morning he'll be here.*

But there had been nothing conditional about it. Her dad was dead, and there was nothing she could do to change it.

"Dad didn't leave Georgia because of Valerie." She was staring out across the yard, too, but she felt the sharp touch of Grandmother's gaze. After a moment, she looked at her. "You know it's true. He left because of Grandfather." He had never deemed Reece old enough to hear the whole story, and all Valerie would say was that he and Arthur had *had issues,* but that was the reason they'd moved to Valerie's hometown of Denver. It was the reason for their infrequent visits and why Dad had little contact with his mother and virtually none with his father.

Plum-tinged lips drew into a thin, hard line, but Grandmother didn't argue. Did she regret that she'd let her husband cost her so much time with her son?

Reece didn't have the chance to find out. Grandmother abruptly stood and started to the door. There she turned back. "Read the book. There will be discussions later."

After leaving Reece, Jones did work on the project for a while, making a few preliminary sketches, compiling lists of plants needed, including virtually every variety of azalea and crape myrtle known to man. It was always fun at this stage, pretend-shopping with someone else's pretend money. The final budget, of course, dictated what they could actually buy, but in the beginning, on a project of this scope, anything was possible.

He had an appointment at one, so he worked with one eye on his watch and about half his senses tuned outside. There'd been no company this morning and, more importantly, no sign of Reece since he'd left her to face her grandmother. He wondered how that chat had gone.

Assuming that someday he got married and had kids, then grandkids, he didn't want to be the type of grandparent who deserved the name of Grandfather. He had one grandpa and one papaw, and either one was good enough for him.

At noon, he knocked off work, drove into town and downed a fast-food burger, then headed north on River Road. His destination was a construction site just north of the turnoff to Fair Winds. His truck bounced over the rutted road that cut through a thick stand of tall pines before opening into a cleared area not visible from the road. White pickups bearing Calloway Construction logos were parked around the site, along with heavy equipment that was gouging up the earth.

Russ Calloway was studying plans spread out in the tailgate of his truck while a huge black dog stood in the bed, front paws braced on the side and head up as if it were supervising the activity.

Beside Jones, Mick straightened and pressed his nose to the window as they stopped next to Calloway. He and the black exchanged looks, then barks before Mick pawed at the door. "Stay," Jones commanded.

Mick didn't look happy about it, but he obeyed.

The machinery made easy conversation out of the question, so Russ gestured to the south, and they began walking that way. Twenty acres of trees had been taken down on the site, and five houses were going in. The construction would be excellent—Calloway Construction was known for top-quality work—and the houses would be expensive, with big lots, swimming pools and room to park monster RVs and boats. The new owners would spend small fortunes having mature trees brought in to replace those dozed down, but not pines. Oaks, likely, maybe a few pecans and sweet gums.

Little work had been done at the southern tip of the site. The ground had been graded a bit, and a brush pile, there fifteen years or more, had been moved, stick by stick, thirty feet away. Sprigs of weed were starting to poke up from the bare earth.

"This is where the surveyor and I found the backpack," Calloway said, gesturing to the new weeds. "It was stuffed in underneath the top layer of brush. Looked like it had been there a long time. It was faded, parts of it rotted."

It was easy for Jones to imagine Glen hiding the pack that held everything he owned. In the weeks they'd camped on Fair Winds—just through the trees and across the fence—they'd routinely hidden their belongings before leaving camp, especially after they'd seen three Howards—Reece, Mark and their grandfather—roaming the woods. They might have gotten caught and chased off, but no one was going to steal their stuff.

"We called the sheriff," Calloway went on. "Once they confirmed that the owner of the backpack hadn't been seen in years, we cleared out the brush pile to make sure…"

That Glen's body wasn't under there, as well. Jones swallowed hard.

"You, uh…know the guy?"

Jones stared at Fair Winds, barely able to make out the crooked pine, barely able to hear the creek. He had asked a lot of questions since he got to town, but all of them about the Howards. No one had reason to suspect his real interest in the area.

Exhaling a heavy breath, he met Calloway's gaze. "I'd prefer people not know for obvious reasons, but... he's my brother. And you're right. The family hasn't seen or heard from him in fifteen years. Not since he was here."

Calloway's expression turned both sympathetic and awkward. "Sorry. We didn't find anything else. He wouldn't have just gone off and left his stuff, I guess."

Jones shook his head. His people were all about survival. Glen could have survived without his belongings, but it wouldn't have been easy. He'd handled those pictures of Siobhan so much that he'd just about rubbed the color off of them. If he'd left Copper Lake, he would have taken them and the backpack with him.

If he were alive, he would have contacted Siobhan.

"Who owned this property back then? Do you know?"

"My grandmother owned it, but it was leased to Arthur Howard. He didn't do anything with it, though. Some Calloway two or three generations before her had leased it to the Howard family for logging. The Howards got out of that business, but they kept renewing the lease." Calloway looked back at the site as if checking on his crew. "My grandmother used to say that Arthur kept writing those checks because he wanted as much land between him and the world as he could get."

Interesting theory. Was the man just antisocial? Or had he had something to hide?

As they started back to their trucks, Jones asked his

next question. "How chatty is the sheriff's department around here?"

"You want to talk to them about your brother without everyone else finding out he's your brother?" Calloway drew a wallet from his pocket, thumbing through it for a business card. It was white, embossed in gold with the badge for the Copper Lake Police Department. "Tommy Maricci's a detective in town. He knows everyone on the sheriff's department, so he can help you out. He'll make sure it stays private."

Jones accepted the card, holding it lightly between his fingers. Seeking assistance from a cop...what would Big Dan think of that?

It wasn't as if he could slip much lower in his father's respect.

He offered his other hand to Calloway. "Thanks. I appreciate your time."

On the way to town, he called the cell number on the business card. Maricci answered on the third ring, sounding distracted. Jones introduced himself, then dropped the Calloway name. It didn't take a stranger more than a day in Copper Lake to realize that the Calloways were important to the area. Their name opened doors or, at least, stirred interest.

They arranged to meet at the coffee shop on the town square. Mick's ears pricked at the mention. Jones had had coffee there every day since coming to town, and every day the pretty barista had given him a treat for Mick, waiting outside.

"You know, she might not be there," he warned. It didn't wipe the anticipatory look from the dog's face.

"I spend more time talking to a dog than I do to people," Jones muttered to himself as he found a parking space down the block. "Of course, most people aren't as smart as you, Mick."

Three small tables occupied a portion of the sidewalk in front of A Cuppa Joe. Jones left Mick at the nearest one while he went inside to order his coffee. He got the plain stuff—dark roast, sugar, one cream. No foam, no ice, no exotic flavorings. Armed with that and a dog biscuit, he returned out front to find that Detective Maricci, identifiable by the shield embroidered on his shirt and the gold one attached to his belt, had arrived and was sharing the table with Mick, who'd climbed into a chair for a better view.

"Pretty dog," Maricci commented.

"Yeah. He gets away with a lot because of that face." Jones showed Mick the biscuit, and the dog immediately sat, his tail thumping steadily. "Sit down there," he commanded, pointing to the ground.

All Mick did was follow the biscuit with his gaze.

Jones set his coffee down, then gave the dog a shove. As soon as his paws hit the sidewalk, he sat again, quivering, and Jones gave him half the cookie.

"My kid responds well to bribes of cookies," Maricci observed.

"Don't we all." Jones settled into Mick's chair and removed the lid from his coffee to let steam escape. Nothing smelled better, he decided, than a freshly brewed cup of coffee.

Except maybe a woman.

"I talked to Russ after you called. So the missing guy is your brother. You have any idea what he was doing out there?"

"Traveling. Camping."

"Did he have a car or was he hitching rides?"

"A little hitching. Mostly walking." Not many drivers had wanted to give rides to two teenage boys, and they'd been wary of the ones who did.

"Do you know for sure he was in this area? Maybe someone stole the backpack elsewhere and ditched it here."

Jones shook his head before taking a sip of coffee. "No. He was here. He told me."

"When was the last time you spoke to him?"

"August 12. Fifteen years ago."

"And what did he say?"

"That he liked this area and was going to stay awhile." There had been more to it than just that. Glen had wanted to stay because of Reece. He'd figured she needed someone on her side if her cousin tried to kill her again. Mark had been scheduled to return home a week later; then, Glen had said, he would leave, too.

Atlanta had been his destination. He was going to get a job and a place to live, then send for Siobhan. Their families would have been appalled that they'd turned their backs on their heritage, even more so over the two broken marriage contracts, but Glen and Siobhan had been prepared for that.

Mark had eventually left, but Glen never had.

"Why didn't your family report him missing at the time?"

"I left home that summer. I didn't know he'd disappeared until the backpack was found. I guess our family thought he'd gone with me, so they didn't know until then, either."

Maricci's gaze narrowed. "Where did you go?"

"I headed out west. About the time I reached the California coast, I turned eighteen and joined the navy. After that, I used the G.I. Bill to get through college and settled in Kentucky."

"You didn't think it was odd you didn't hear from your brother all that time?"

Jones's smile was more like a grimace. "I haven't heard from any of my family. The one time I went home, my father closed the door in my face. Every time I call, as soon as my mother recognizes my voice, she hangs up. The only exception was when she told me Glen's backpack had been found."

"So your family took your leaving hard."

Tension knotted Jones's gut and turned the coffee bitter. Carefully he set the cup down, leaned back in his chair and laced his fingers together. He was about to admit something he hadn't told anyone in fifteen years and hadn't really believed he ever would. But if it helped find out something about his brother… "The address on Glen's license was North Augusta, South Carolina, but we actually lived in Murphy Village. Just off the interstate, big houses, trailers, lots of statues of the Madonna. Are you familiar with it, Detective?"

Just for an instant, Maricci showed surprise—something, Jones would bet, he didn't often do. Quickly his expression went blank again, and his tone was perfectly neutral when he spoke. "What law-enforcement agency in the region isn't? So you and your brother…are…were Irish Travelers."

Watching traffic on the street, Jones swallowed hard, then absently reached down to slip the second half of the biscuit to Mick. Touching the dog's fur, feeling him breathe, hearing his gung ho crunch, eased him a bit.

Then he forced his gaze back to Maricci's. "Yes. But that's not what Glen was doing here that summer. It had nothing to do with the family business." *Business* included just about every scam a man could think of: resurfacing driveways, putting on new roofs, sell-

ing stolen property, construction. Wheeling and dealing and stealing.

There was an art to the business, Big Dan always
said. A man needed charm and sincerity, an ability to
bullshit and a little bit of acting. The men hit the road
in spring and stayed gone into fall, always doing business far from home. They didn't run cons where they
lived—another of Big Dan's rules.

"It's my understanding the older boys travel with the
men. Why weren't you and Glen doing that?"

"We asked for one summer off to do whatever we
wanted. We'd always done what we were told to. We
were good workers. Glen had already quit school, and
they'd decided I'd finished my last year, too." He'd
gotten one more year than his brothers and most of his
cousins, but it hadn't been enough. He'd wanted to learn
more—to learn a different life. "Our family agreed to
it."

"And you used the time to get the hell out of the
South."

Jones nodded.

"Was Glen planning to go back?"

"No." Grimly Jones recounted his brother's plans,
leaving out mention of Siobhan by name. She'd gone
through with the arranged marriage—to one of Jones's
cousins—and had a half-dozen kids. Most likely, no
one even suspected she'd intended to run away, and
he'd prefer to keep it that way. Glen had found enough
trouble. No use spreading it to her.

"How long was he here?"

"A few weeks. Three, maybe."

"And the last time you saw him—where was that?"

"Right around where the backpack was found. He'd
made camp and was going to stick around awhile. I

went on without him." The biggest regret of Jones's life. If he'd stayed…

"What was his routine? Did he keep to himself? Hang out in town? Did he try to pick up a few dollars somehow?"

"We stayed out of town as much as possible. If there was fishing to be done, we did that. If there was a creek to swim in, we did that. We didn't mess with people." His jaw tight, he deliberately disregarded the last question. He and Glen had saved as much money as they could for the trip, and their father had given them some, but, yeah, they'd stolen when the opportunity was too good to resist—cash a few times, food a few others. They'd both wanted to live more law-abiding lives, but they'd been willing to do whatever was necessary to get to those lives.

Maricci was quiet a moment, then he pushed his chair back. "I'll talk to the sheriff's investigator who caught the case. Where are you staying?"

"Fair Winds. I'm putting together a bid to restore the gardens there."

"Really. I've heard about those gardens from my grandfather. He said people used to drive out there just to look through the gate at them." His gaze turned speculative. "What does Miss Willa's grandson think of the plan?"

"He's not thrilled, or so I've heard. I expect to hear from him sometime soon."

"I expect you will. I'll be in touch, too." Maricci stood, offered his hand, then gave Mick a scratch before walking away.

## Chapter 5

After an excruciatingly stiff dinner with Grandmother and Mark, Reece retired to her room upstairs for a little light reading. The book she'd been instructed to study lay open on the bed, about as interesting as a six-month-old newspaper. The writing was as pretentious as the title—*Southern Aristocracy: The Howards of Georgia*—and the musty odor was giving her a headache.

Restlessly she got out of bed and went to the windows. The nearly full moon cast its eerie light, giving a ghostly glow to the objects it reached directly, casting deep shadows elsewhere. Out front, except for distant lights across the river, everything was dark. On the side, a lone light shone on the patio, but the cottage was in darkness. Everyone was asleep but her.

There had been more talk at dinner about the garden project, Mark trying repeatedly to get her to side with him. She hadn't, which had frustrated him, but he'd continued to argue his case until Grandmother had flatly told him to shut up or leave.

After that, conversation had fizzled out. He had asked a few halfhearted questions about her life in New Orleans, talked a bit about his daughter, then murmured on his way out, "Thanks for the support, Clarice."

After the door had closed behind him, Grandmother had drily repeated, "Yes, thanks for the support, Clarice."

*It's none of my business.* She hadn't said the words out loud, but she'd shrieked them inside.

As she stared out the window, movement caught her attention in the shadows across the driveway. She squinted, trying to find focus in the lack of light. Was it merely leaves rustling? A bird fluttering past? Maybe Mick, out for a middle-of-the-night bathroom break.

She couldn't make out anything, and trying just made her head hurt worse. With a sigh, she began to rub her temples, but her hands stilled as a thud sounded downstairs.

It was likelier one of the resident ghosts than Grandmother. Still, after a moment, she started toward the door. She would really rather lock herself inside, crawl into bed and let the book bore her to sleep, but there was no lock on the door, and what if it *had* been Grandmother? What if she'd gone downstairs for something and fallen?

Opening the door, she looked quickly down the hall. Grandmother's door was closed, but that didn't mean anything. It was always closed.

She stepped into the hallway and softly called, "Grandmother?"

No response from upstairs, but the quiet click of a

door came from below. Just as the bedroom doors were always closed, the doors downstairs were always open, except the kitchen door…and the one that led to Grandfather's study. Reece took the few steps necessary to reach the top of the stairs, then crept to the landing, where the study door became visible, and the hairs on her arms stood on end.

Faint light seeped out underneath the door, and distant footsteps shuffled. Unable to breathe, unable to do anything at all but cling more tightly to the stair rail, she watched the shifting light as those footsteps paced slowly to the left, then slowly back again. *One, two, three, four, five…*

Maybe it was Grandmother. Maybe she felt closer to Grandfather in his study than anywhere else, so she went there when she couldn't sleep.

But to convince herself of that, Reece would have to go down the stairs, across the hall and open the door.

She couldn't.

*…six, seven, eight, nine…*

Chills swept over her, creating shivers that left her barely able to stand. She wanted to throw her stuff in the truck and drive home without stopping. She wouldn't feel safe again until she was curled up in her own bed with Bubba, Louie and Eddie all snuggled close.

Abruptly the footsteps stopped and the light winked out. The house seemed unnaturally quiet, all the normal sounds gone. There was the light rasp of her breathing, the thudding of her heart and nothing else.

She couldn't say how long it took to steady her legs or to uncurl her fingers from the banister. Afraid to turn her back on the study door, she backed up the steps and down the hall, pivoting when she reached her room. She closed the door noiselessly, leaned against it and gave a great exhalation.

When she breathed again, she caught the faint hint of tobacco smoke on the air. Her stomach knotted once, then did it again as her gaze took in the book she'd left open on the bed, closed now and resting on the dresser. Then, slowly, she looked upward to the message barely visible on the mirror.

*Go away.*

It appeared as if it had been written on wet glass, fading as the moisture dried. Even as she watched, it disappeared, not leaving so much as a smudge behind.

Which resident ghost was the message from? Was it friendly advice…or a threat?

Moving to the bed, she shoved her feet into a pair of flip-flops, then hastily left the room again. She tiptoed down the hall to the back stairs—anything to avoid the area around the study—then switched off the patio light and let herself out the side door. Moonlight was illumination enough for her tonight.

It was a little too cool for the thin cotton shorts and T-shirt she wore as pajamas, but she didn't care. Out here she could breathe. She could think. She could feel, if not safe, then saf*er*.

As she settled in one of the chairs with her back to the house, her shoulders sagged with release. It wasn't her first encounter with a Fair Winds ghost. She hadn't been in danger. Someone was just telling her to do what she very much wished she could: say goodbye to this place forever. If the message had been a threat, any ghost could have come up with more ominous words.

If it was just a warning, though, it could have at least said *please* or *for your own good.*

Or someone could have just been making mischief.

A weird sense of humor in life would likely follow its owner into death.

Across the road came a little creak, and her muscles started tightening again before she saw Mick leap off the cottage porch and trot toward her. There was no other sign of movement from the place; she guessed Mick had awakened Jones and he'd let the dog out and was waiting half-asleep inside.

"Hey, sweetie," she murmured, offering a scratch to the dog.

He put his paws on her leg, stretched up and licked her chin, then hunkered down again, practically vibrating with pleasure as she rubbed the base of his ears and down his neck. He reminded her of how very much she missed her dogs. They were probably all stretched out on her bed right now, snoring loudly, pushing against each other as they rambled in their dreams.

"I wish I had a treat to give you, but I haven't trespassed into the kitchen yet. I don't know if Lois would mind, but there's no doubt that Grandmother would." She'd found the kitchen the most welcoming room in the house fifteen years ago, and Inez, the housekeeper then, the most sympathetic person. But once Grandmother had caught her slipping in there, both Reece and Inez had been warned.

Mick didn't seem to mind affection in place of treats, so she continued to rub him, leaning forward as he slowly sank onto the ground, then rolled onto one side to expose his belly.

"Don't forget you already have three at home. You can't have mine, too."

She startled, but just a bit, nothing like the scare she'd already had. Jones did indeed look only half-awake. His hair was mussed, he wore the same shirt and shorts he'd worn on their walk that morning, and his feet, like hers, were in flip-flops.

"I'm not trying to win over your dog."

"You're doing a pretty good job of it for not trying." He sank into the nearest chair and propped his feet on the fountain rim. "I wondered what was taking him so long. I should have known. If there's a pretty girl with magic fingers around, he forgets it's the middle of the night."

*Pretty girl.* The warmth that settled over her was far too much response for the casual compliment.

"Sorry I kept him out." But she wasn't. She'd needed the peace Mick provided, even it was just for a few minutes.

"Trouble sleeping?"

"Yeah, a bit."

"I never have trouble sleeping. Mick doesn't snore, but he does have this loud, rhythmic breathing when he sleeps. It just kind of draws you in. I'm usually out ten minutes after he is."

"Lucky you." Though, usually, falling asleep wasn't her problem. The rude awakening from the nightmares was. Nothing like a few bloodcurdling screams to put the end to a much-needed rest.

"I saw your cousin leaving after dinner. He didn't look like a happy man."

That was a good description for Mark, at least on the subject of the garden plan. He'd told Grandmother he was worried and didn't want anyone taking advantage of her. Grandmother had retorted that it was her *money* he was worried about, not her, and not to worry, that she wouldn't let *anyone,* including her grandson, take advantage of her.

"Has he talked to you yet?" Reece asked. "Tried

to send you away or make it worth your while to convince Grandmother you can't fit her into your schedule? Or maybe he'll decide she can have a smaller—much smaller—garden."

"Not yet. He's probably checking out his options. First he'll try to change her mind. When that fails, he'll either bring in other family members—"

Reece interrupted with a snort that made Jones grin.

"—or talk to his lawyer to see what legal steps can be taken."

"He mentioned Grandmother's lawyer." The thought of that kind of interference irritated her. Having been married to Grandfather for fifty-some years certainly entitled Grandmother to spend her money on anything she wanted, even if it was clowns performing every day in a combination water/skateboard park on the front lawn. "Has it really come to legal action on any of your jobs?"

"Just once, in Florida. Old man with grown children and a new bride. He left the bulk of his estate to his kids, but the wife got to spend pretty freely while she lived. The kids insisted she was trying to bleed the estate dry to punish them. The thing is, the kids were going to get about $20 million each, and they paid their lawyers more than the project was budgeted for to fight over the cost of a five-acre garden."

Uncomfortable in her crouching position, Reece sat up, then scooted to one side before patting the seat. Mick crawled up with her, the front half of his body across her lap. "Twenty million dollars. Wow. You could do a lot of good with that kind of money."

"Not those people. Money had never made them happy, and it never would."

Had money made Grandmother and Grandfather

happy? Did it make Mark happy? After considering it a moment, Reece decided she couldn't reconcile the notion of her grandparents and happiness. They just weren't the smiles-and-joy type.

Mark, on the other hand… He'd always had money and had taken it for granted. She would bet the idea of not being wealthy had never crossed his mind; it was literally unthinkable. And, like many overindulged children, he'd grown into an adult for whom, apparently, the more he had, the more he wanted.

What about Jones? She watched him, gazing into the darkness. "Does money make you happy?"

His gaze flickered to hers, and a thin smile touched the corners of his mouth. "Money's important. I won't deny that. There have been times, back when I was in college, when I could barely pay my rent or buy groceries, and the last few years I've made more than I can spend. I definitely prefer the extra cash. But there's a lot more to being happy than that."

"So *are* you happy?" It was a nosy question, too personal to ask someone she'd known less than forty-eight hours. Valerie would admonish her; Grandmother would remind her that Howard women never pried. But Jones was free to ignore the question or tell her it was none of her business. She wouldn't be offended.

He was quiet a long time, as if it wasn't an easy answer for him. Finally, he exhaled loudly. "Yeah, I guess. For the most part."

What parts of his life was he unhappy with? Besides his estrangement from his family, what would have to change to make his answer a simple *Yes, I am?*

He turned the question back on her. "What about you? Are you happy?"

"Yes," she said immediately, then, feeling a flush of

guilt for not being totally honest, she added, "For the most part. I, uh …" She looked at him, then focused her gaze on the dog settled so contentedly in her lap. "I don't get along with my mother, I'm not close to my grandmother and cousin, and I'd like to get married and have kids someday though I've never met anyone I'd remotely consider tying myself to. But other than that and…that summer, yes, I'm happy. I like my job. I love my dogs and my friends. I can pay my bills, and I'm in good health. That's a lot."

Halfway through her response, his gaze had zeroed in on her. She could feel it as surely as she felt Mick's warm, comforting weight against her.

"What happened that summer?" His voice was low and comforting, too, with its blend of accents. It was a perfect voice for talking in the dark, for lulling an edgy woman into relaxing all those taut muscles, for making her feel safe.

God, she'd been using that word a lot lately. Yearning for something she couldn't regain until she faced the fears that had taken it from her.

Unless remembering stole it from her for good.

Jones watched her, her fingers lightly stroking Mick's fur. Her head was tilted so little of her face was visible to him, but that was enough in the silvery light to know that her expression had gone blank. The suspicions that had reared their ugly head that morning came back, prickling his spine, making him sit straighter in the chair.

He thought she wasn't going to answer and didn't blame her at all when slowly she lifted her head and met his gaze. "I don't know."

"What do you mean?"

She shrugged. "I don't remember most of the time I spent here. I remember coming with my mother. Mark arrived soon after we did for his summer visit, and Valerie left again not long after that. She didn't even tell me goodbye. I got up one morning, and she was… gone. The next memory I have after that day, she and I were back in Colorado."

Truth? It was impossible to tell with an accomplished liar. But something about the look on her face, the way she said the words…it *felt* like truth.

He knew from fifteen years ago that her mother had just bailed on her. She'd told Glen the story, and he'd repeated it angrily, wondering how a woman could do that to her child. In their culture, family came first… unless two restless sons ran off to experience a different life.

"Where did she go?" he asked, though he knew the answers to that, too.

"Grandmother said she left to take care of things back at home, but she was gone a long time. There wasn't that much to take care of."

That had been Miss Willa's first explanation. Later, she'd told Reece that her mother had gone to Europe with friends. Glen had shaken his head in disgust. *Can you believe that? Leaving her own kid to go on* vacation?

"What did Valerie say when you asked her?"

Reece's brow furrowed. "She would never talk about it. Even now, if I ask her anything about that summer, even about my father's death, she says the past is past and she's not going to waste any time discussing it."

That was cold, when your daughter still had questions. *If* the daughter really did have questions. But leaving your grieving thirteen-year-old daughter for whatever reason was pretty damn cold, too.

"So you really don't remember anything? Swimming in the creek? That old cemetery? Hanging out with your cousin?"

She shook her head. "I remember enough from the first few weeks to know that Mark and I didn't hang out. He was mean."

*Mean* wasn't the half of it.

If she was being honest, she didn't remember Jones and Glen.

She didn't remember Mark trying to drown her.

She didn't remember anything her grandfather might have done to her.

She had no answers to give him.

She was of no use to him.

*If* she was being honest.

He could be honest even if she wasn't. He could tell her why he was here, what he remembered of that summer. He could appeal to her conscience, could trade answers to some of her questions for some sort of closure for the family regarding Glen.

Silently he snorted. If Glen was dead, knowing was better than not knowing, but it wouldn't provide closure. It wouldn't make the knowledge any easier to bear. It damn sure wouldn't ease his guilt for leaving his brother there. Yeah, Glen had been older; yeah, he'd been stubborn as a mule. But Jones should have stayed with him. After that threat from Mark…

It had been such spoiled-juvenile bluster. *I'm gonna tell my grandfather that you're trespassing out here, and he'll call the sheriff to put you in jail.*

Reece, dripping wet, eyes huge and still shaking

from her near-drowning, had gotten in his face. *You say a word, and I'll tell him you tried to kill me.*

Mark had put on a good show of bravado—*He'd never believe you over me. He loves me, not you!*—but his voice had quavered and a look of pure panic had come into his eyes before he'd run off through the woods.

None of them had believed he would really tell, or have the nerve to confront either Glen or Jones again.

The whisper of cushions and a grunt from Mick drew his attention back to Reece, shifting to a more comfortable position. As soon as she settled again, so did the dog, looking utterly content.

"Did I mention that I had a visit from a ghost tonight?" she asked, the lighter tone in her voice signaling the end of the other subject.

"It must have slipped your mind. What happened?"

"Just light. Footsteps. A book moved from where I'd left it a few moments before." She paused. "A note written on the mirror telling me to leave."

"Not a very friendly ghost, huh."

She shrugged carelessly, though Jones wasn't too convinced by it. "Maybe he doesn't like sharing my room with me. Or maybe he thinks if I couldn't bother to visit while he was alive, I'm not welcome now that he's dead."

"He? Your grandfather?"

She shrugged. "I smelled tobacco. Though I doubt he's the only Howard who liked his cigars."

The presence at the creek that morning had smelled of tobacco, too. Arthur Howard had dominated the place while he lived. It was no surprise he'd hang around now.

"You planning to spend the night out here instead of inside with him?"

She made a *pfft* sound. "If Grandmother had a chaise with a nice thick cushion on it... He didn't waste any time on me when he was alive. I doubt he'll give me much more of his attention now."

"That would be my guess." Jones yawned, then nudged Mick. "Come on, boy, I need to get some sleep."

He half expected the dog to open one eye, give him a blank look, then close it again. Instead, Mick stepped lightly to the ground, stretched, then trotted for the cottage. Reece laughed at his fickleness. "Yeah, good night to you, too, Mick. You're welcome for all the scratching."

"Sitting with you is comfortable," Jones said as he stood. "Stretching out on the bed, though, is his idea of the way to spend a night. See you tomorrow."

He crossed the road into the shadows that hugged the other side, listening for some sound that Reece was going inside, too. It didn't come. When he stepped inside the cottage, he turned back to fasten the screen door and saw her still sitting there.

He intended to lock up, strip down to his boxers and crawl back into bed, but the sight of her held him there. She seemed so alone and vulnerable. She *was* alone: no family that counted, no man to stand beside her, just friends back in Louisiana.

That wasn't too different from his life, the cynic in him scoffed, and he wasn't alone or vulnerable.

But no one had abandoned him. No one had ever wanted him dead.

After a few minutes, she stood and, like Mick, stretched. Her back arched, her breasts pushing against her thin shirt, the hem of the shirt rising up over her middle. She held the position long enough to make his mouth dry, then straightened, looking at the house for a time before finally walking to the door. She really didn't like the place. But why should she, when all the memories were bad?

He stood there in the dark, just watching, until she disappeared inside. A moment later the patio light came on again. Soon after that, a shadow appeared in the only room lit up, then those lights went out, too.

Rubbing at the unease cramping his neck, Jones closed and locked the door and went to bed.

Reece awoke even more tired than when she'd finally fallen asleep. She hadn't had any screaming-to-wake-the-dead nightmares, but her sleep had been restless, her dreams haunted by Grandfather's fierce scowls, Mark's taunts and angry words.

*If you say a word...*
*Curiosity killed the cat.*
*Meee-oww.*

She felt a little better after a long shower. After dressing in jeans and a shirt, she picked up the family-history book from the dresser, her gaze fixing on the mirror. Leaning forward, she blew out her breath on the glass, curious to see if the message might reappear in the fog. It didn't.

Grandmother had already eaten breakfast and was in her study, her back to the door, when Reece tried to slip past. Without glancing up, she said, "It's about time you got out of bed."

Reece grimaced before turning into the room. Grandmother could hear the faintest creak of a floor-board when someone was trying to sneak past, but never heard any of the thumps and thuds from the ghosts. How was that? "Good morning."

The old lady turned, and displeasure wrinkled her nose. She disapproved of jeans—Reece had heard that on her first day in the house fifteen years ago—and shorts—Reece had learned that on her second day. And she *certainly* disapproved of Hawaiian shirts with bright red flowers on a royal-blue background.

Some days a girl just had to dress to suit herself, and today Reece really needed the lift from the vividly colored shirt.

"I'm going to a meeting in town today," Grandmother said once she was certain the censure had been recognized. "As Mr. Jones is going to restore the gardens, I believe joining the garden society is in my best interests. The meeting is today, and there will be a luncheon afterward. I gave Lois the day off, so you'll be on your own for lunch."

"That's fine." Reece wasn't a fan of eating out by herself, but this would give her a chance to go into town and see if anything jogged her memory. She doubted it, since the bulk of her time had been spent here on the property, but hey, it was an excuse to get out for a few hours, right?

Grandmother tucked her handbag under one arm and bypassed Reece on the way to the door. When her gaze fell on the book Reece held, she gave a firm nod of approval.

Reece followed her into the hall. "Do you need a ride?"

"Of course not. I am fully capable of driving myself where I want to go." Grandmother cast a sharp look over one shoulder. "I may be approaching eighty, but I'm as able-bodied and sharp-minded as ever."

Her snippy tone made Reece draw back emotionally if not physically. "I never suggested you weren't."

"Your cousin suggests it quite regularly."

"He worries about you." Heavens, she was defending Mark. Who would have imagined it.

As she stepped outside, Grandmother shot her another scowl. "When he's got something genuine to worry about, I'll tell him."

When the warm morning sun struck her, Reece felt a moment of relief. A gentle breeze blew from the west and smelled faintly of wood smoke. On the far side of the river, a thin plume of smoke circled lazily into the sky, and an unseen boat putted on the water. It seemed such a normal scene that, for a moment, *she* felt normal.

As Grandmother passed the fountain, heels tapping on the brick, Reece drew her attention back. "I only offered because I hadn't seen a car around."

"It's in the garage, where we've always kept the cars."

Garage? Reece glanced around, her gaze lighting on the storage sheds that stood between the house and the barn. She'd walked right past them yesterday, paying them no mind, but now she saw the keypad on the nearest one, and the overhead door.

A faint memory stirred: that door standing open, Grandmother's big old Cadillac gone, Grandfather's beat-up pickup inside. The tailgate was down, the bed littered with dirt and holding a tarp stained with something dark and wet. Grandfather, filthy and sweating, yelling at her to get back to the house, and Mark…just standing there, a look on his face. Fear? Excitement?

Goose bumps covered her arms, and she shivered violently, hugging herself to ward off the sick dread.

She'd seen that feverish, gleaming expression in Mark's eyes before, one day when he'd...when she'd...

The memory was there, so close, so elusive. She focused inward, trying to grab it before it slipped away, but she was too late. Like fog struck by burning sun, it disappeared.

Like the message on the mirror last night.

"Do you intend to follow me all the way?"

Grandmother's impatient voice brought her back to the moment. They were halfway to the garage, when Reece couldn't remember crossing the patio. She looked at the garage, then back at the house, and gave herself a mental shake as she stopped. "No, of course not."

"The spare key and the code to the gate are on my desk. If you go somewhere, be sure to lock up. And if you do go somewhere, change clothes. Howard women do not appear in public dressed so gaudily."

Reece stood where she was, book clutched in her arms, until the garage door had lifted, until Grandmother had climbed behind the wheel of a big old Cadillac—Lord, surely not the same one she'd driven fifteen years ago—until she'd backed out of the garage and driven past with a frown directed at Reece.

"Wow. That car's a classic. It's older than both of us."

Jones's words would have startled her if Mick hadn't run into view the instant before he spoke. She turned and watched the two of them saunter down the road from the direction of the barn.

He wore shorts again, denim, with a T-shirt advertising a nursery in Louisville. His hair was untidily combed, and dark glasses hid his even darker eyes. He looked friendly, approachable, sexy—and still, somehow, mysterious. It wasn't the way he moved, all smooth and easy, or the way he grinned, all open and boyish. It was just some aura about him. Some little bit of *something*.

"Everything else around here is ancient. Why not the car?" She greeted Mick with a quick rub, then asked, "Walking the property again?"

"Giving Mick some exercise. He'd sleep twenty-two hours a day if I'd let him." His gaze slid over her. "I like your shirt."

Glancing at the huge flowers, she smiled. "Me, too. It's hard to take life too seriously when you're wearing a Hawaiian shirt." If only that were true.

"Where is Miss Willa off to?"

Reece fell into step with him and headed back the way she'd just come. "She's joining the garden club in town. Now that you're restoring the gardens, it's her duty."

"She takes duty very seriously."

"Yeah." Except the duty of caring for her granddaughter when she'd taken her in. Had Grandmother been so disinterested that she hadn't noticed that something was wrong? Or had she just preferred Mark? After all, she'd described Reece as spoiled with a tendency to cry, while Mark was merely a pest.

"You've got a book again."

*Again?* He'd never seen her with a book. Oh, but she'd told him she'd read a lot that summer. "It's a Howard family history, bought and paid for by the Howard family."

"Lots of unbiased views and straightforward facts, huh."

"There's nothing like having total control over the final product. How's the work coming?"

"Great. I've done some preliminary sketches, and Lori, who works back in the office, is doing a search for the original statuary. I doubt we'll be able to buy much of it back, but Miss Willa wants to try. We're also putting together a list of—"

He stopped in his tracks, the words stopping, too. Reece looked at him, then in the direction he was staring: his pickup. It took her a moment to realize what was wrong with the picture: both tires on the driver's side were flat.

"Son of a bitch!" Jerking off his glasses, he lengthened his stride and Mick ran ahead, a low rumble coming from his throat.

When Reece caught up, she saw that the other two tires were flat, as well. With a jerk of his head, Jones muttered, "Yours, too," and she spun around to the same sight with her SUV.

"They weren't flat when Mick and I left the house. What about you?"

"I don't... I was talking to Grandmother, and I—I remembered something from—from before. I didn't notice the cars at all."

His gaze sharpened, and she realized his eyes were the biggest source of his mysterious aura. They were so dark, so intense. A lot of emotions could hide there. A lot of secrets.

He started to speak, but bit off the words and yanked his cell phone from his pocket instead. Finding the number he wanted, he gripped the cell tightly and walked a few feet away. "Hey, Calloway, it's Jones again. I just have a request this time." Tersely he explained the situation, said thanks and disconnected. "He's going to send a wrecker out."

Reece frowned as she walked toward her car. She'd heard the Calloway name before, and not just on the plantation she'd passed on her way here. Memory clicked: Mark had mentioned it. Grandmother's lawyer.

Why would Jones have Grandmother's lawyer's number in his cell?

"Robbie Calloway?" she asked, her voice reedy. "The lawyer?"

"No. Russ Calloway. Owns the biggest construction company around here."

She didn't realize she'd been holding her breath until she let it go. It seemed logical a landscape architect would meet the owner of a local construction company. Maybe Jones did a few small jobs on the side while working on big projects like this.

He passed her, walking a wide circle around her truck. "Your ghosts ever do anything like this before?"

She lifted one shoulder in a hapless shrug. "One of them moved my book last night. Have yours?"

He shook his head. "I've never run into a destructive one." He gazed up at the sky, rested his hands on his hips and flatly said, "Well, hell."

*Well, hell,* indeed.

# *Chapter 6*

The tow-truck driver gave them a lift to a tire store in town, the one recommended by Russ Calloway. After talking with a service technician, Jones and Reece left their vehicles there and walked outside to the sidewalk.

"You hungry?"

When she didn't answer right away, he turned to see her staring around intently. There was nothing re-markable about the block: a '50s-era drive-in; Charlie's Custom Rods; a window treatment place; a chiropractor's office. Was she looking for something recognizable from fifteen years ago?

Or was it all recognizable?

"Reece," he said, and her gaze flew to his. "You want some lunch while we wait?"

"Uh, yeah. Sure."

"You have a favorite place here?" He half expected a

terse repeat of the claim that she didn't remember anything, but he didn't get it.

"No."

"Downtown's that way." He pointed, and they started walking to the nearest northbound street. "There are a couple places down here to eat—a deli, a steak house, a home-cooking diner, Mexican, pizza, a riverside place that's a little more upscale than the others. What do you feel like?"

"Any place where I don't have to sit up straight on the edge of my chair and deal with a full complement of silver."

"Miss Willa still likes things a little formal, does she?"

Her scowl was her only response.

Copper Lake was a nice little town, laid out around a central square with a white gazebo, lots of flowers and the usual war monuments. He pointed out a couple of businesses as they walked the few blocks to the square, then stopped across the street from the Greek Revival mansion that sat just southeast of the square.

"That's where your grandmother is. The garden society meets there."

Reece looked at the house, then back at him. "How do you know that?"

"My job basically boils down to gardening. I learn these things."

"Beautiful place."

"The oldest house in town. Not rumored to be haunted, though I assume it is."

She looked at the house a moment longer, its white paint gleaming in the morning sun, the massive oaks with their Spanish moss casting welcome shade. It had been meticulously restored a few years earlier and was ready to face the next two hundred years with grace.

When Reece glanced back at Jones, her expression was troubled. "Do you think someone sneaked onto the grounds this morning and slashed our tires?"

"I didn't see any slashes." Or any footprints, though gravel wasn't likely to show much. "I'll bet they just let the air out."

"They who?"

He shrugged. "Ghosts? Your grandfather? Your grandmother?" A pause for effect, then, "You. Me."

Her face paled. "I didn't— Why would you—"

"I didn't, either." They crossed the street, passed A Cuppa Joe and continued northward. "I just can't see Miss Willa stooping to vandalism. For someone to come onto the property, he'd either need the code for the gate or would have to climb the fence, and in the middle of the morning, that's a bit of risk for very little gain. It isn't much of a warning. It isn't violent. Mostly it's just a nuisance. Why would a living, breathing person bother?"

A few yards passed in silence.

"Mark has the code," she said quietly.

"I figured that. And if he was seen, he'd have an excuse: he'd come to check on Miss Willa. But why? Like I said, it's not a big deal. If the tires had been slashed—" and he could see Mark doing that, quick, vicious work "—that would be different. We'd be out the money for new ones, and there's some element of threat there. But just letting the air out?"

She nodded as if agreeing as they turned at the next corner. Their destination, a little diner he'd found his first day in town, was in the middle of the block, a place that looked every bit its age. There were rips in the vinyl benches that had been repaired with duct tape, and the industrial carpeting on the floor carried a lot of stains. But the rest of the dining room was clean, the waitresses friendly and the food good.

He waited until they'd settled in a booth and the waitress had taken their order before he brought up the subject niggling at the back of his mind the past hour.

"You said this morning that you'd remembered something from before." He watched for a response and saw it in the clenching of her jaw, the shadowing of her eyes. "You want to talk about it?"

She looked as if she wanted to put it out of her thoughts forever, but after a sigh, she shrugged. "It wasn't anything much. Just I'd gone outside one morning and wandered over to the garage. Grandfather and Mark were in there, doing something with his pickup, and he...he *screamed* at me to get back in the house. He was angrier than I'd ever seen him. And Mark was so complacent."

Disappointment shafted through Jones. She was right: it wasn't much. From what he knew, Arthur had always been angry around her and Mark had almost always been a smug little bastard.

But if she recovered one memory, then the others could come back, as well.

And when she remembered him and Glen? How would she feel about him not telling her right up front who he was and what had happened? She would be pissed off. He didn't care. He could handle pissed off. He couldn't handle not knowing what had happened to Glen.

"What was the old man's problem with you?"

"I don't know. My dad moved away when he was in college—met my mother, finished the semester and transferred to a school in Colorado, where she was from. He hardly ever came back here." Her expression was mocking. "Howards didn't leave Georgia. This was where they belonged.

"But I think it was more than that. My dad was a good guy. People liked him, respected him. He got along with everybody. He was a high school teacher, and even his students loved him. But he couldn't get along with Grandfather. Even when we did visit, they rarely spoke."

"So Arthur extended his estrangement from your dad to include you?"

She shrugged, and he was struck again by the air of vulnerability. Every kid, he'd guess, wanted affection from their family. How did it feel when you couldn't have it, and not even because of something you'd done? Just because of who you'd been born to? Jones missed his family like hell, but he'd known he would lose them when he left the life. He'd considered the consequences a long time before he'd taken the action. And if he had a kid who wanted to know his grandparents, aunts and uncles, they would welcome him. They wouldn't hold Jones's sins against him.

"What about your mother's family?"

"Her parents died before I was born. No siblings, two uncles who traveled around the world on business. She hardly knew them, and I've never met them."

"Wow. Your family really sucks."

. Her laughter surprised her as much as him. "I've got good friends. They're better than family."

The waitress brought their lunch, a silent invitation to lighten the subject. They talked about inconsequential things as they ate—a few of his more interesting jobs, the shop where she worked, their dogs.

They were trading funny dog stories when a newcomer to the diner stopped halfway to the counter to stare at them. Mark Howard.

He smiled when he saw Reece, then his gaze shifted to Jones, and though the smile remained, the warmth didn't. He turned cold enough to give a man the chills if he was the sort whose blood ran cold. Jones wasn't.

"Well, you're the last person I expected to see in town today," Mark said, his words directed to Reece but his gaze on Jones. "What brings you out?"

Some of her warmth drained away, too, replaced by stress that darkened her eyes. "Grandmother had a meeting and gave Lois the day off, and I needed to come to town, so..."

Mark frowned at the mention of Miss Willa's meeting. Afraid she might be with her lawyer drawing up a contract for the garden project? But he apparently decided to let it pass as he turned his attention to Jones. His gaze was steady, like a snake, his expression blank.

Did Mark recognize Jones? How could he forget the faces of either kid who'd stopped him from killing his cousin, especially the one who'd knocked the snot out of him? Especially when, back then, no one told him no and got away with it. Maybe he was waiting to see if Jones acknowledged him first, or willing, if Jones was, to pretend they'd never met.

Or maybe he really didn't recognize him. Maybe he'd dismissed Jones and Glen as nuisances who'd temporarily gotten in his way, who weren't worthy of a place in his memory fifteen years later. Maybe the snakelike look was for Jones the garden designer trying to do business with Miss Willa, not for Jones the kid who'd once thwarted him.

He came closer, his intent to sit down showing

when he'd actually lowered himself to Reece's bench. A shiver danced up her arms and she slid, in record time, to the far end of the bench, giving Mark plenty of room. She didn't relax, either, Jones noted, when he left plenty of that room between them. She was trying to hide it, but she still looked trapped.

"So you're the gardener looking to part Grandmother from her money."

Jones picked up his glass, rattling the ice in the tea. He didn't bother to correct his occupation—that would just let Mark know he'd gotten to him—but instead said evenly, "I'm the one she approached about her project."

"You don't feel guilty?"

"For what?"

"Entering into a deal with a senile old woman."

Jones would have coughed up tea if he hadn't already swallowed. "Little woman? Five foot nothin', ninety pounds if that? White hair, sharp gaze that doesn't miss a trick? Proper and determined and stubborn as hell? I just want to be sure we're talking about the same woman, because there's *nothing* senile about the one I'm dealing with."

Color tinged Mark's cheeks. "'Senile' was a bad word choice." Before anyone could ask him what word he would substitute, probably digging himself a deeper hole, he went on. "You have to admit this plan of hers is ridiculous. She's almost eighty, for God's sake. Spending all that money, and for what? Some silly gardens that don't belong that she might not even live long enough to see completed."

"I don't think it's ridiculous at all. The gardens were there longer than they've been gone. To most historians, Fair Winds without its gardens is just a shadow of its former self."

Mark snorted. "I don't give a damn what most historians think. It's not their property. It's not their money."

Very quietly, still pressed against the wall, Reece said, "It's not yours, either."

Mark turned his scowl on her. "Of course you're siding with Grandmother, trying to get back in her good graces." Then his gaze shifted between them, turning speculative. "Or is there more to it than that? Isn't it a coincidence, the two of you showing up here at the same time, him wanting to take thousands of Grandmother's money, you encouraging her every step of the way?"

Just the accusation was enough to turn Reece's cheeks a guilty pink in spite of her rigid denial. "I'd never met Jones until the day Grandmother introduced us."

Which Mark knew, of course, was a lie. Jones watched anger ripple through the other man as he struggled to control it. Mark may have grown up. Adult responsibilities and a family of his own may have made him regret the sins of his youth. He may have become a better person, one who matched the stories Jones had heard since arriving in town.

But he still had that sense of entitlement.

And he still had that temper.

"Never discount the power of fate," Jones said mildly, drawing Mark's attention back to him. "I've always been interested in the Fair Winds gardens, since I was a kid. And Reece's, ah, friend was the one who persuaded her to come back now."

"Friend?" Mark echoed.

She forced an almost natural smile. "My psychic advisor."

For a long time Mark simply stared at her. Then he

laughed. It was unexpected and hearty and broke the tension at the table. "You see a psychic? Does Grandmother know that? Oh, my God. When Macy was pregnant with Clara, she went to a psychic here in town just to find out if everything was all right, and Grandmother about pitched a fit. You'd've thought she'd had a voodoo priest kill a chicken for her and drank its blood, the way Grandmother carried on."

"Grandmother doesn't know everything," Reece replied, "and she doesn't know Evie."

Mark dragged his fingers through his hair. "Look, I'm sorry. I don't like this whole idea. Grandmother brought it up while Grandfather was alive—repeatedly—and he was adamantly against it. He hated those gardens enough to destroy them, and whatever his reason, I think we should respect his wishes. Just because he's passed is no reason to forget everything he said." His gaze moved to Jones. "And it *is* a hell of a lot of money. And she *is* old. I just hate to see…"

"What about respecting Grandmother's wishes?" Reece shifted on the bench to face Mark.

The question flustered him. He seemed to take good care of Miss Willa, as much as she needed it, but he'd always been closer to Arthur, Jones remembered. It was Arthur Mark had complained to, Arthur who encouraged him to think he was lord of everything and everyone around him.

Arthur he'd threatened Jones and Glen with.

Mark sat silent a long time, his expression growing more chastened by the moment. At last, after clearing his throat, he spoke. "Of course Grandmother's wishes matter. It was just *so* important to Grandfather that Fair Winds remain the way he left it."

"Why?" Reece asked.

Mark smiled ruefully. "Damned if I know. I just know he hated the gardens. He hated flowers in general—wouldn't have them in or around the house. I always thought maybe it had something to do with his father's death, because he tore out the gardens right after Great-grandfather passed. We didn't even have flowers at his funeral. Grandmother ordered that all arrangements be sent to the old folks' homes in town instead."

Arthur had been fairly young when his father died—twenty-four or twenty-five—Jones reflected. The old man, if he remembered the history right, had died one day in the garden—heart attack or stroke, no one had been sure. Arthur had been the one to find him, toppled over on a freshly replanted bed. If they had been very close, if the flowers had reminded Arthur of the heartbreak of that day…

Jones supposed it was a plausible explanation. His uncle Kevin had never been able to eat fried chicken again, his wife's specialty, after her death. People handled grief in different and sometimes odd ways.

"I know Grandmother loves flowers. I just don't see why she can't be satisfied with a normal garden plot, like everyone else."

"Grandmother's never been satisfied with 'normal' anything. She's not like everyone else, you know. She's a Howard."

The dry tone of Reece's voice drew Jones's gaze. He'd bet his entire business that all she'd wanted in life was normalcy: father, mother, home, extended family. With the exception of her father, she'd gotten anything but normal, to the point that she'd basically written off her family and made a new one for herself with friends.

How hard had it been for her that summer, having to be a Howard and never getting it right?

Harder than it had been for Jones to be a Traveler. At least his family had loved him. The men in the family had taught him how to do everything except abide by the law, and the women had spoiled him. He'd disappointed them, but because of what he wanted, not who he was.

Reece had never been a proper Howard; it wasn't in her. And her grandparents hadn't let her forget it.

Mark's sigh was heavy and resigned. "I just hate…"

To see Miss Willa bury Arthur's wishes with heavy equipment, stonework and an entire nursery full of flowers? Or to see that money leave the family coffers? A bit of both, Jones suspected.

And it was going to be a hell of a lot more than just thousands. Jones didn't work on the budgets—Lori oversaw that—but he could give a ballpark figure for a project of this size. The final number, to do everything Miss Willa wanted, would knock ol' Mark flat.

Though most of Jones's clients rarely got exactly what they initially wanted. Even among the very wealthy, there were usually compromises.

Mark exhaled again. "All right. I'll accept Grandmother's wishes. I don't approve, but as she so succinctly pointed out, it's not my business." He stood, but paused before walking away. "Hey, Clarice, will you tell her I can't make it tonight? Macy's got some kind of mommy's night-out thing tonight, so I've got Clara. Since Grandmother believes small children should be seen and not heard, and Clara insists on being heard all the time, they don't spend much time together."

"I'll let her know."

With a grim nod, he went to the counter, picked up a foam container and left.

"I wondered how Grandmother got along with her great-granddaughter," Reece commented as she settled more comfortably on the bench. "It doesn't surprise me that she doesn't."

"She's not big on displays of affection."

She shook her head. "The first time we visited here, she was waiting for us on the patio. She air-kissed my mother, gave my father a stiff little hug, then looked down her nose at me, told me I was to refer to her as Grandmother—not Grandma, MeMe or anything else—and recited the rules for residence at Fair Winds, however temporary the visit might be. No running, roughhousing, loud play, interrupting, picking at food, raising one's voice, disturbing the adults..."

"So the first thing you did was go inside and shriek, 'Where are the ghosts, Daddy?'"

She smiled, unaccountably pleased that he'd remembered her comment from the morning before. "I can't tell you how many times during that visit he had to say 'She's just a kid' to all of them—Grandmother, Grandfather and even Valerie. And it wasn't an acceptable excuse to any of them."

Jones's features softened, reminding her again of how handsome he was. Watching him sitting there across from Mark, she'd been struck by their differences: total opposites, hard versus soft, tough and indulged, independent and very dependent, easygoing and quick to rile. By Howard standards, Jones was surely nowhere close to Mark's exalted status, but by *this* Howard's standards, he was head and shoulders above.

He was drop-dead-sexy handsome. He loved his dog.

He'd been nothing but friendly to her and respectful to Grandmother. And when he smiled…

He did it now, well aware of her scrutiny and amused by it. "You want to sit here while we wait for the garage to call, or would you prefer to see more of the town?"

"Let's hit the town." Maybe she would see something or someone that would jog loose another memory. And it would be harder for her to stare at him while they were moving.

Though he offered to pay her tab, she did so herself and he let her without arguing. She liked that.

Back outside, they turned west, strolling along the sidewalk toward the river. She gazed at storefronts and into offices, wondering if she'd ever walked this sidewalk before. Had she played in the square or been inside that beautiful house Jones had pointed out? Had she accompanied Grandmother on shopping trips to any of these stores?

The questions made her head hurt. For the thousandth time, she wished she were like most other twenty-eight-year-old women: average, everyday, with total recall of an average life. And for the thousandth time, she reminded herself that she wasn't.

Realizing that they'd covered nearly a block in silence, she grabbed at the nearest sight—twinkling diamonds in a jewelry-store window display. "Are you married?" The minute the question was out, it struck her as odd that she hadn't asked sooner. She'd just assumed he was single. Something about him—she couldn't even say what—gave the impression that he didn't have a wife and kids waiting back in Kentucky for him, that he wasn't missing a part of himself.

Not that all married men missed their wives. But

her father had, and she just had this sense that Jones would, too.

"No. Never have been."

"Why not?"

"Same reason as you. I've never met anyone I'd want to go home to or hate to be away from."

She kept her gaze on the store windows as they walked, too often catching a glimpse of his reflection in the glass. "Do you want to be someday?"

"I always figured I would. Isn't that kind of what we're taught to expect? We grow up, we get married, have kids and grow old." He shrugged, and his shirt rippled in the window glass.

The street they were on ended at River Road. One block to the left was the square; to the right were the types of businesses that seemed to line the main road out of any town. Straight ahead, starting next to the last building, was a park that filled the narrow space between river and road. She headed that way.

As parks went, there was nothing special about Gullah Park: no flower beds or fancy playgrounds. At this point, there wasn't even a parking lot, though a clearing to the north looked as if it might be for that purpose. There was just neatly mown grass, tall live oaks whose massive branches spread in every direction and a paved path for runners. She walked to the edge of the river, lowering herself to a cushion of grass, her toes just inches from the water.

Jones leaned against a tree branch that dipped so low it required man-made support to stop its own weight from crashing it into the river. Hands shoved in his pockets, he watched her.

She watched the lazy current and breathed deeply of the damp, earthy, fishy smell. "Each time we visited

Grandmother, Daddy took me fishing outside the main gate of Fair Winds. He was happier outside than in. We never caught anything—we splashed around too much for that—but it didn't matter. He said fishing wasn't about catching fish. It was about peace and quiet and freedom."

Jones pushed away from the tree and sat beside her. "Trust me, when you're hungry, it's about catching fish."

Resting her arms on her knees, she tilted her head just enough to see his face. "Have you been hungry?"

"A time or two. Not in a lot of years."

She looked back at the river. It stretched half a mile to the western bank, dotted with condos and large houses. There was a bridge to the south, nothing but water and trees to the north, save a boat anchored in the middle. Though a fishing pole was mounted on the side, the fisherman appeared to be snoozing.

"What happened between you and your family?" The words came out so softly, and he remained so still beside her, that she wasn't sure he'd heard. She'd decided she wouldn't repeat the question because it wasn't any of her business when he moved, just the blur of a shrug in her peripheral vision.

"They wanted me to continue with the family tradition, and I wanted something else. Like your dad. He wanted to do something, be something, other than a Howard, like all the men before and after him. Tradition was fine for my grandfathers, my dad, my brothers, but I wanted...more."

"And they've never gotten over it."

"Some things you just don't walk away from."

Family was one of those things. Some people who did it managed to salvage some sort of relationship, but she didn't think her family would. Her grandparents had never forgiven her dad for wanting something else; her grandmother wasn't going to forgive her for cutting them off. And if she was brutally honest, she'd never forgiven Valerie for abandoning her to her grandparents, or her grandparents for the way they'd treated her.

She stared harder at the boat. The man inside was slumped back, a floppy hat shading his face. A red-and-white cooler occupied the other bench, and the same colors bobbed on a plastic float, marking his line in the water. "Do you regret it? Would you go back and change things if you could?"

"I regret a lot," he said evenly, "but no. I wouldn't live the way they'd wanted me to. I couldn't."

What was it they'd wanted of him? Was his family like her grandparents—dedicated to a way of life so superior in their minds that nothing else was acceptable? Had it been a matter of occupation, religion, military service? When people were narrow-minded enough, stubborn enough, the slightest disagreement could become an unbreachable gulf.

"You mentioned brothers. How many?"

A shadow crossed his eyes. "Three brothers, two sisters."

"Wow. And all of them did exactly what was expected of them, which made your rebellion even harder."

"Yeah." He might have gone on, but at that moment, his cell phone went off, a straightforward *ring-ring.*

You could tell a lot from a person's ringtones, she thought, comparing that to the three she heard most often: "Marie Laveau" for Evie, "Witchy Woman" for Martine and an *uh-oh, trouble* dirge for Valerie.

The call was short, and Jones stood up as he disconnected. "That was the garage. The cars are ready." He extended his hand to her, and she took it without thought, as if it were the most natural thing in the world. But what happened next wasn't natural at all.

His hand was warm, the skin callused. His fingers closed snugly around hers, sending heat and tingles and something that felt very much like *life* seeping upward, through her hand, along her arm, into her chest. The sensation was both relaxing and disturbing, but in a thoroughly pleasant way. Awareness. Connection. Intimacy.

And he felt it, too. It was in his startled gaze, in the way his breath hitched. He stared at her, and she stared back, surprised, anticipating…*something.*

Moment after moment they remained that way: him standing, her sitting, hands clasped, gazes locked, barely breathing. Slowly his muscles flexed, and her body responded. He pulled her to her feet, so they stood toe to toe, still staring. His scent blocked the river's as she breathed hesitantly, then deeper, filling her lungs with his warm, steamy fragrance. She couldn't say whether she leaned toward him deliberately or if it was primal attraction.

She *could* say that it took all her strength to stop, no more than a fragment of space separating her mouth from his. He raised his free hand, his fingertips almost touching her cheek, but he stopped, too, before making contact.

And the moment ended. She dropped her gaze, backing away, and he lowered his hand, also backing off. When their intertwined hands tugged, he hastily let go, flexed his fingers, then shoved both hands into his pockets again. "We, uh…"

Her head bobbed like the fisherman's float on the river. "Yes, we should."

"I, uh…"

"Yeah, me, too."

They walked from the river to the garage in silence.

Even that wasn't uncomfortable. When was the last time she'd walked three or four blocks with a man in complete silence without casting about almost feverishly for something to say? Never.

But she didn't need to say anything to Jones. She had plenty to think about, plenty to just feel…satisfied and curious about. That moment, that touch…and it had been a *touch* of far more than just hand on hand. It had been important. Intimate. So full of potential. Not once had her brain whispered a warning, a reminder that she couldn't get involved, that she needed answers before she could go blithely trusting anyone.

All true—at least, in the past. Still true now, except that something basic inside her, maybe the very core where her emotions lived, wasn't showing much interest in listening this time.

When they reached the garage, both their vehicles were parked to the side, with the same old tires, newly refilled with air. They paid the bills, then Jones walked to her SUV with her.

"Are you headed back to Fair Winds?"

"I'm going to drive around a little bit. See some of the places Grandmother says we used to go."

"Since you're not going home yet, I've got a couple things to take care of. If you get home before Miss Willa—" he headed around the SUV to his own truck, then looked back at her "—be careful."

# Chapter 7

Jones waited in his truck until Reece had turned east out of the parking lot, then he headed south, his destination the biggest nursery in Copper Lake. He wanted to check the quality of the plants, get a feel for the operation. Miss Willa had stressed that she wanted him to buy locally wherever possible, and to hire locally, as well. Part of the Howard obligation to the community, he supposed.

The plant farm was just the other side of the city-limits sign, spreading along the road for a half mile and farther than that away from it. He pulled into the gravel lot and parked, only then becoming aware of the Jag behind him. He got out of his truck and waited as Mark parked, then climbed out.

"I was on my way back to the office after an appointment when I saw you. I hope you don't mind that I followed you." Mark removed sunglasses that probably cost more than Jones's entire outfit, including his favorite top-quality work boots, and gestured in front of their vehicles. "Can we talk?"

Outdoor tables, chairs and fireplaces were clustered in small groups in the section ahead of them, some on squares of grass, some on tile pavers, some on concrete patios. Mark chose a teak set occupying a tiled area, with a fireplace built of the same stone. The cushions were comfortable, warm from the day's sun, the prices posted excessive. Of course, not many customers could lay the patio and build the fireplace themselves, like Jones could, saving at least half the price.

Mark took a few moments to settle comfortably in the armchair, then he blurted out, "You remember me."

Then Mark remembered, too. It was nice to know that Jones had made such an impression back then. "I do."

"So why did Clarice say she'd never met you before Grandmother introduced you?"

It wasn't Jones's place to answer that question truthfully, especially when he didn't know the truth. Reece's claim of amnesia—real or scam? If it was true, who else knew that was why she returned? Was it a secret? Or had she already told Miss Willa, who probably would pass it on to Mark?

"She prefers Reece."

Mark blinked. "What?"

"She goes by the name of Reece."

"Huh. Can't say I blame her. Macy didn't want to name our daughter Clara, but some version of it—Clara, Claire, Clarice—has been in the Howard family for generations. Macy has called her Clary since she was born. Says it's a much better name."

He was silent a moment, his face softened by mention of his wife and daughter. He might be a Howard, Jones thought, but at least he knew how to show affection. He wasn't the sort who would avoid his own grandbaby because she was too noisy for his tastes.

Then Mark's expression turned puzzled. "So…why did Cla—Reece lie about knowing you?"

Jones could offer any number of answers: *I don't know. Ask her. It's not my place to tell.* But if he gave any of those answers, the next logical action for Mark would to be ask Reece herself.

And when—if—she denied it, his next logical statement: *You hung out with him and his brother for weeks that summer. They rescued you when you almost drowned in the creek. How could you have forgotten them?*

And if he was being really truthful: *I was the one who almost drowned you. His brother took care of you, and Jones damn near drowned me before he finished punching me.*

Then he'd threatened them. Jones had left town, and Glen had disappeared.

If Reece truly didn't remember, Jones would prefer to keep himself in that black hole of traumatic forgetfulness. No matter what the reason for his deception, she had some deep trust issues. She wouldn't take it well.

The last thing he wanted was Mark tattling around Fair Winds about Jones's presence on the farm fifteen years ago. Who knew how Reece would react? Worse, who knew how Miss Willa might react? And since Reece hadn't asked him to keep it between them…

He shrugged. "From what I understand, she doesn't remember much about that summer. Losing her father that way…" *To say nothing of being abandoned, end-*

*lessly criticized, tormented, possibly molested and almost killed.* She had plenty of reasons for forgetting.

Mark stared. Counting his blessings? Thinking that was one less thing he needed to apologize for? Wondering if Jones himself was the real threat here, and not the garden project he was starting?

"And you haven't told her?" He sounded part dismayed, part satisfied.

Jones shook his head. She deserved answers, but he'd come here for his own answers. Her remembering the details of an ugly summer just didn't stack up against his finding out what happened to his brother. How he died. Where he was buried. Why.

Whether it was his fault.

Keeping his gaze focused on Mark, he said, "I'm more interested in finding out about Glen."

"Glen...the other boy." Mark sounded fuzzier in his recollection of Glen. Of course, the three of them had only had that one run-in, and Glen hadn't bloodied his knuckles on Mark. He'd been on the sidelines calming a hysterical Reece.

"He left that day, didn't he?" Mark asked. "I never saw him again."

"Neither did I," Jones said flatly.

"I never knew his name." Sheepishness crept into his face. "Never knew yours, either, until Grandmother told me she'd hired you and then I saw you this morning."

Mark murmured the name again, frowning, then shook his head. "All that talk about telling Grandfather and him calling the sheriff... I never did. I was just... embarrassed and upset. I'd never meant to hurt Cla— Reece. I was just messing with her—I always messed with her—and suddenly there you were and things got out of control. I *never* would have hurt her."

An explanation with more than a little finger-pointing. Jones called the memory to mind: him and Glen on the way to the pool, where Glen was meeting Reece while Jones went on to the river to fish. Hearing splashes, cries, agitated enough that they'd broken into a run. Seeing Reece in the water, her cousin's hands on her shoulders, pushing her down while she clawed her way up, shrieked, then went under again. Mark wearing a look Jones had never seen on anyone—fierce, angry, driven.

He and Glen had both jumped into the water, Jones grabbing Mark under the arms and jerking him away while Glen pulled Reece up sputtering and half dragged, half carried her out of the water. His victim gone, Mark had turned on Jones, landing several punches before Jones subdued him, then dragged him out a safe distance from Glen and Reece.

Mark had been spitting mad, livid at their interference, then abruptly, the viciousness disappeared and the anger became that of a boy, all but swallowed up in fear at the magnitude of what he'd done.

Things had been way out of control before Jones and Glen had arrived, but if that was what Mark needed to tell himself to live with his memories…

"I kept waiting on her to tell Grandmother," Mark went on. "I couldn't eat or sleep, and I kept my distance from her as much as I could. She never said anything, but she never trusted me again." Then he scoffed at himself. "She never trusted me before that. I'd been spending summers with our grandparents since I was five years old. It was *my* time, and I *hated* having to share them with her. It sounds selfish, but I didn't know her dad, so it's not like his death should have ruined my whole summer. I was such a jerk."

Jones didn't bother agreeing with that. "When did her mother come back?"

"A couple days later. She just showed up, no phone call, no nothing, and had the housekeeper pack Reece's stuff. As soon as Inez was done, they left. We never saw Reece again until now."

"Where had she been?"

"Aunt Valerie? Supposedly taking care of business, then vacationing, but..." Mark's mouth thinned, then he went on. "My father and his brother weren't close, and my mother never did care much for Aunt Valerie. I heard her tell Father once that she thought Valerie's vacation had been more of the very discreet rehabilitative kind than the spas-and-fun kind."

Jones considered that: a less-than-responsible woman, based on Reece's comments, suddenly widowed, finding it difficult to cope, especially when her mother-in-law and the housekeeper were there to take care of her child. Needing a little help to get to sleep and a little something to keep her steady when she was awake, to keep the enormity of her loss at bay. How easy it would have been to rely too much on pills prescribed by a helpful doctor and/or liquor that was readily obtained, to the point that rehab quickly became a very real necessity.

That would explain why no one had told Reece the truth. If Valerie had deteriorated that quickly, she wouldn't have wanted her daughter to know—*still* didn't want her daughter to know. And Miss Willa couldn't fudge and tell Reece her mother was sick and needed hospital care; that would have terrified a kid whose father had just died. Miss Willa was of an era where family secrets *were* secrets. She hadn't considered the psychological damage to Reece, believing she'd been abandoned by her only parent.

Mark glanced at his watch before rising. "I'd better get back to the office before my assistant—" His cell phone interrupted his words. He glanced at it, muted it and returned it to his pocket. "Your friend, Glen...you think he might have stayed around here? Is that why you took this job?"

"One of the reasons." Jones stood, too. "I'm pretty sure he never left the area."

There was no significant change to Mark's expression. No worry, fear, anxiety. The possibility apparently meant nothing to him. "I came back every summer until college, but I pretty much kept to Fair Winds. I wanted to spend as much time with Grandmother and Grandfather as I could. But if he's in Copper Lake, he shouldn't be hard to find. Just ask around."

The cell phone rang again, and he frowned. "I've got to go. Thanks for your time."

Jones watched him leave, then headed away from the furniture and into the broad aisles flanked by shrubs, containers in trees and flowers. He'd always given himself credit for good instincts; all Travelers, especially the men, relied on them. But his seemed more than a little dull this afternoon.

Did he believe that Reece really had amnesia from that summer? Maybe. Had the scene in the creek really been horseplay that got out of control? Stranger things had happened. Was Mark really a changed man? Who knew what a man was really like inside?

But he couldn't quite shake the memory of that look in Mark's eyes. The same cold look in the pictures Jones had seen of Arthur Howard.

Being surrounded by plants usually put him on an

even keel. He liked the smells—flowers, earth, fertilizers. They spoke of potential, beauty and the cycle of life. He could plant a garden now that, with a little care, would still thrive long after he was dead, or trees that would still grow strong and straight long after his great-grandchildren had died. He could leave a mark.

But today he wasn't finding much of a sense of balance. The back of his neck itched, and an unsettled feeling kept slithering up and down his spine. An unknown person—or ghost—had let the air out of eight tires. A ghost had moved the family-history book—significant in itself?—and left a message on Reece's mirror.

Mischief? Warning? Threat?

*If you have any trouble with the ghosts when you start digging up the yard...*

*Grandfather* screamed *at me to get back in the house...*

And the echo of words Jones had used himself a few moments ago: *family secrets.*

Doing a 180, he headed back toward the parking lot. He could check out the nursery tomorrow. Right now he felt the need to return to Fair Winds.

And Reece.

Twenty minutes of driving around town gave Reece a good visual of Copper Lake. She located the hospital, the shopping mall, schools and probably most of the churches—and bars—in town. She even found the Howard church, recognizable from the huge addition fifty years ago paid for by and named in honor of the family.

She parked across the street from the church and sat on a bench that fronted a well-kept cemetery. Generations of Howards had attended the church, including her father—although not Grandfather. But there was no reminder of them in the marble and granite markers spread across the ground. All Howards were buried in the family plot at Fair Winds.

Except for her dad.

"I would have thought if you took the time to visit a cemetery, it would be the one where your own family is located, to say nothing of changing into appropriate attire before the visit."

Reece refused to feel guilty about her Hawaiian shirt and jeans, but when she lifted her gaze to Grandmother, she found herself automatically straightening her spine and shoulders as if she were dressed in her finest clothing.

"Of course, even if you did visit the family cemetery, you wouldn't find anything of your father beyond a marker, thanks to your mother."

*Ghosts rarely haunt cemeteries,* Jones had said, but attached to people or places important in their lives. Fair Winds hadn't been important to Elliott in his life, so it didn't matter in his death.

"Valerie carried out Daddy's wishes."

Grandmother *humph*ed. "Cremation, then scattering his ashes in *Colorado*... Never in the history of the Howard family—"

"It was what he wanted."

Reece's interruption earned her a tight-jawed look. "Death rituals are for the living, not the dead. It didn't really matter what he wanted."

That certainly explained Grandmother's refusal to be swayed on the garden project by Mark's insistence that it went against Grandfather's wishes.

Or maybe she'd just spent so many years giving in

to Grandfather's wishes that she'd decided it was time for her own wishes to matter.

She seated herself on the bench, facing the opposite direction. "Why are you here?"

"I came to look at the church."

"So you're sitting with your back to it."

Reece started to swing one leg to straddle the bench, decided against the criticism sure to follow and stood to turn around properly. "I remember it a little." Stiff dresses, shoes that pinched her toes, best behavior, a little white leather-bound Bible with her name engraved in gold.

She couldn't recall ever seeing the Bible again after that summer.

Granted, she'd never gone to church again, either. Valerie had liked sleeping in on Sundays.

"Your father's memorial service was held here. Can't rightly call it a funeral without a body, not even ashes." Grandmother scowled at the steeple atop the church. "Cecil's funeral was held here, also, as well as your grandfather's. If you'd like to visit their graves, you know where the family plot is."

Reece didn't admit to her visit with Jones the day before. She certainly didn't admit that her only interest in Grandfather's grave was making certain he was in it.

Abruptly, Grandmother stood, more energetically and gracefully than most women half her age. "It's time to go. Come along. You can follow me home."

Reece considered refusing just to be difficult, but what was the point? She'd seen everything she wanted in town, anyway, finding few memories of any substance, and all of them from her first month there.

The answers to that summer were at Fair Winds, with Grandmother, Mark, maybe even with the ghosts.

She stayed a comfortable distance from the Cadillac on the short drive home, then pulled into her usual space while Grandmother parked right beside the patio. Jones's truck wasn't in sight, but clearly he was home, since Mick lay curled on a sunny spot of patio, the warm stones of the fountain at his back. He opened one eye to identify the newcomers, then closed it again, unconcerned.

"You there," Grandmother said, opening the Cadillac's trunk as Reece crossed the road. "You can unload these flats."

Reece blinked, never having been referred to as *you there* by the oh-so-proper matriarch of the Howard family, then by the reference to flats. Had one or more of her tires been vandalized, as well?

Then Jones stood up in a shady spot of the patio, laying aside a laptop, and Reece saw the contents of the trunk: flats of pansies in yellow and blue, the shades ranging from palest pastel to vibrant, deep hues. The trunk was full, and a glimpse showed the backseat was, as well. Had pansies had a place in the Fair Winds gardens of old, or was Grandmother planning her own touches?

If so, Jones didn't seem to mind as he lifted the first box out. "Beautiful. Good, healthy plants."

"The garden society sells them as a fundraiser. Of course they're beautiful and healthy."

The snippiness in her voice didn't seem to bother him at all as he carried the flat to a protected corner of the patio. Reece watched him walk away, the light load no strain on his muscles, the long steps no strain, either, on his long, lean legs. When he turned but before he caught her watching him—she hoped—she shifted her purse under one arm and bent to pick up one of the flats herself.

Grandmother stood in her way. "Really, Clarice. Let the people who are paid to do the dirty work do it."

Some little devil made her imitate the tone. "Really, Grandmother. People who belong to garden societies tend to get their hands dirty in the garden. And you know what?" She leaned closer, lowering her voice. "It washes off."

Sidestepping Grandmother and Jones, whose grin disappeared before the old lady could see it, she deposited the flat beside the first, laid her purse on a table and came back for another.

Disapproving, Grandmother stood by and watched as they completed the unloading. "The beds nearest the front porch were always planted with pansies in the fall," she announced. "I realize it will be a long time before the entire garden is completed, but I'd like those beds done now. As I'm sure everyone's realized, I may not live to see the final results, but I will have flowers in this yard for at least one season."

She unlocked the door, then came back around the fountain, giving Mick an irritated look before pressing the keys into Jones's palm. "Return the car to the garage—the code is the same as the gate—then send the keys back to me with my granddaughter."

Reece might have been embarrassed by Grandmother's imperiousness if she hadn't become used to it so long ago. It was part of the Howard superiority over everyone else. Daddy hadn't had a drop of it in him and hadn't tolerated it from Valerie, either, but after his death, Valerie had proven almost as adept at it as Grandmother.

"Want to ride along?" Jones asked as he opened the driver's door with a sweeping gesture.

She didn't want to climb into the Cadillac where, unseen by their grandmother, Mark had so often pinched and poked at her, and she really didn't want to go to the garage. But she agreed, anyway, sliding underneath the steering wheel and across the bench seat to the passenger side. Jones was just a breath behind her, filling the space with broad shoulders and adding his scents of sun and cologne to the aroma of fresh earth and plants.

The drive took all of thirty seconds. Jones pressed the electronic opener clipped to the visor, and the door lifted with a slow creak. The lightbulb overhead provided just enough illumination to make the space shadowy, cavelike, creepy. Goose bumps raised along her arms, and she suppressed a shiver by keeping her gaze firmly settled on Jones's hands. Grandfather was dead. She wasn't thirteen. She could handle this.

Especially with Jones an arm's length away.

He eased the Cadillac into the space, squarely in the center. When he shut off the engine, the silence was overwhelming, the structure shadowier, creepier. Her mind's eye saw that old pickup, Grandfather and Mark, the truck bed holding clods of dirt, something wet—oil?—and a tarp-covered lump. And, in a voice as real as her own, she heard Grandfather's roar: *Get back in the house* now!

Chest tightening as it had that day, she fumbled with the door, then, too clumsy, she scrambled across the seat and climbed out the driver's side so fast that she slammed into Jones's solid back.

The impact knocked him a step off balance, but he recovered and reached back, taking hold of her arm,

steadying her beside him. "You in that big a hurry—"
His tone was light, to match his expression, until his
gaze connected with hers. She must have looked as pan-
icky as she felt, because his expression sombered and
he led her out into the warm afternoon sunshine, not
stopping until twenty feet of gravel and grass separated
them from the garage.

"Are you okay?"

She nodded, not yet trusting her voice.

He studied her a moment longer, then asked, "You
want to let go of me, or would you rather wait a minute?"

For the first time she realized her hands were
clenched around his arm, her fingertips whitened from
pressure. She tried to let go, tried to smile, to shake off
the reaction, but all she managed was a faint whim-
per. That was enough to bring him closer, his free arm
wrapping around her, pulling her until her body was
snug against his, his voice a quiet murmur above her
ear. *It's okay. I've got you. It's okay.*

Heat seeped into her, and security and comfort. After
a moment, the shudders faded, leaving her muscles tight
and exhausted. The chill faded, too, and the echoes of
Grandfather's shout. Her pounding heart slowed, her
legs steadied, her fingers unclasped and she thought
inanely how different a nightmare was, even a waking
one, when you had somebody to hold you and chase it
away. After her father died, she'd never had anyone...
until now. Until Jones.

She looked up at him and found him staring back,
concern making his already dark eyes even more so.
His other arm now loosed of her grip, he raised his
hand, brushing one finger over her face, fluttering her

eyes shut, skimming her cheek, feathering over her lips, as if he were wiping away the fright.

Then he bent closer still and kissed her. It wasn't the hottest kiss she'd ever had, or the hungriest or the sweetest, but it was the best, because she needed it, and he knew it.

After a long, gentle moment, he raised his mouth, his forehead resting against hers. "Better now?" Soft words, tender.

This time she managed a real smile, if somewhat shaky...though this time, the shakiness was from the kiss, the taste and feel of him, rather than fear. "I am."

Then *she* kissed *him*. She didn't warn herself off, didn't tell herself that this was a bad time and a worse place for any kind of intimacy. She didn't let herself think at all.

She just acted.

And he *re*acted.

Jones was no idiot. He knew it was possible for a kiss to go from nothing to burning-hot-need-to-get-naked in half a second, but he still wasn't prepared for it. Hell, he hadn't been ready for Reece to initiate a kiss at all. She'd needed calming, and that was what he'd offered: a hug and a nothing little kiss to settle her fears.

And now he was combusting from the outside in. His tongue was in her mouth, his erection pressed against her, his hands cupping her face while her hands roamed all over him. His blood pumped hot, fire licking along his veins, his only thought *now!* and his only need privacy. The cottage was closest and his befuddled brain was trying to direct his body that way, without losing contact with her body, when some small, still-functioning part of his brain spoke up.

"Miss Willa," he mumbled against Reece's mouth, trying as he spoke to put some space between them. It was hard when he didn't really want that space, and neither did she, judging by the way she clung to him.

His words, though, did the trick. Her hands still on his chest, one beneath his shirt, she drew back enough to focus her gaze on him. "When a man brings up my grandmother while I'm trying to kiss him senseless, I'm obviously not doing it right." Her voice was husky, tinged with amusement and tempered with impatience.

"I passed senseless a while ago." He tried for a rueful grin and thought he succeeded with the rueful part. "We're not exactly being discreet, and your grandmother would give you hell for dallying with the hired help."

She looked at the house, where rows of windows stared down on them. Jones hadn't been inside yet, but he'd guess they could be seen there beside the driveway from at least two-thirds of the structure.

"She's given me hell plenty of times before," Reece said, taking a step back, then another. "It wouldn't be anything new. But she wouldn't fire you for dallying with her granddaughter."

The thought hadn't occurred to him. Once voiced, it gave him a moment's thought: leaving Fair Winds knowing no more about Glen than when he'd come.

But Reece was right, and it showed in her smile. "It'd be easier to send *me* away than to find another big-name landscape architect to handle her project." There was only the slightest hint of self-pity in her voice before she went on. "A name that I think, after getting more intimately acquainted, I should know."

He left her a moment to return to the garage and

close the door, then came back, took her hand in his and started toward the house. "You know my name."

"Jones. No *Mister*. Just Jones." She gave him a wicked sidelong glance. "Don't tell me your first name is Justin. Or Justice."

"Nope. Though that wouldn't be so bad."

She laughed at the idea of something worse than Justice Jones. "I don't even know whether Jones is your first or last name."

She'd asked him that twice, fifteen years apart. The first time he'd always been on the lookout for trouble, and never giving anyone his full name, or sometimes even his own name, had been one safety measure. The second time he'd thought she knew who he was.

Now he believed she didn't. He'd been wavering on the subject of her self-claimed amnesia, but at that moment he admitted he believed her. And she was right; after that, uh, intimacy, she deserved to know that much.

"It's my last name. My first name is between me, my lawyers, my accountant and my mother. Everyone else in the world just calls me Jones."

"Even your girlfriends?"

"When I have one."

"Do they get tired of waiting for you back there in Kentucky while you travel all over working?"

As they got closer to the house, he released her hand and, in silent agreement, they put a few extra inches between them. "You're assuming they all break up with me. That's not always the case. Besides, long-distance relationships aren't so tough anymore, not with the internet, smartphones and the money to make regular visits."

"Yeah, it worked for your grandparents and parents."

"And without the internet, smartphones or airlines."

"Is that what you want? A long-distance relationship? To always be saying goodbye, sleeping alone, waiting for the next visit? Putting business first, wife and kids last?" Scrunching her face into a frown, she shook her head. "You're no romantic, Jones."

Now it was him laughing. He'd learned all the gestures—the fancy restaurants, the flowers, the extravagant gifts, the celebrations for no reason. He could romance a woman with the best of them. It wasn't his idea of fun, but if it was what a woman wanted, and if he wanted her, he could do it.

He didn't think the gestures were what Reece wanted at all. Just genuine emotion. Knowing she was important and being shown in the ways that really mattered— the little ways. A massage. A shoulder to lean on when she was upset. A voice to ease the fear. Loving her dogs unconditionally.

Oh, yeah, and being there every night at bedtime.

"First, I'm talking about just a relationship at the moment, not marriage. And second, it's not ideal, but life usually isn't. Ideally, I'd want a wife who shared my interest in the business, who would travel and work with me. And ideally by the time we had kids, the business would be at a point where I could just run it and let other people do the traveling."

"If you're known well enough in this business to impress Grandmother, then you're in that position now," Reece pointed out as they reached the patio.

"I am," he admitted, then parroted her own words back to her. "I've never met a woman I'd remotely consider tying myself to. At least…not yet."

Their gazes locked, and again there was heat, need, hunger. It was sexual tension, he told himself. Lust.

Any man in the world who'd just shared that kiss with her, whose nerves were still humming with little electric shocks, would feel the same way.

It didn't mean she could be that woman. It didn't mean they could share any sort of relationship beyond a temporary one. It didn't mean she felt or wanted the same thing.

It didn't mean a damn thing at all except that he was in sorry shape.

"I—I'd better get the keys back to Grandmother." Reece's voice was unsteady again, just a little quaver that hinted of her physical response.

"I'd better start on the front bed." He handed her the keys and watched her go to the door. There she turned back to watch him until finally he forced himself to move.

Pansies. Flower beds. Mulch. Soil. Edging. Hard work.

Exactly what he needed.

# Chapter 8

The clock in the hall chimed four o'clock, drawing Reece's gaze from the book. Grandmother was resting, something she'd done every afternoon as far back as Reece could remember, and the house was particularly quiet with the housekeeper gone.

*Quiet* didn't apply to outdoors, though. Shortly after she'd come inside, Jones had driven past on his way out. An hour later, he'd returned, parking the truck in the middle of the driveway about even with the porch. Yes, she'd gone into Grandmother's study to peek through the lace curtains. Behind him was another truck, bigger, loaded with pallets of brick and mulch, bags of concrete mix and some type of equipment. He and the driver had unloaded, shaken hands, then the truck left and Jones turned to the front yard.

The equipment—a tiller, she guessed, not that she'd ever had the opportunity to need one—was noisy and distracted her from her reading. She'd finished four chapters of *Southern Aristocracy* without remembering a word.

Now she closed the book and sighed loudly. It echoed in the salon, as if a dozen souls joined in. Setting the book aside, she stood and stretched, looked around as if seeking something else to do, then gave up the pretense and went into the hall. A slight hum from the refrigerator, the swish of paddle fans in the salon and Grandmother's study, the smells of wood polish and age and... Her nose twitched as she looked toward the front hall. She took a few steps toward the heavy closed door and sniffed again.

It was cigar smoke. Not the stale decades' worth of smoke Grandfather's study had seen, but fresh, almost sweet. She imagined as she stared at the door that she could even see the faint curl as the smoke escaped the room.

She took a few more steps, reaching the door in fits and starts. For a time she just looked, aware that everything in her had gone cold. The smoke was definitely seeping under the door in delicate wisps as if drawn out by an invisible vacuum.

Fingers trembling, she touched the door, solid ancient wood, neither warm nor cold, just a door. Slowly she slid her hand down and to the right, until her fingers brushed the intricate brass knob that the sea captain Howard had brought from India. She could turn it. Open the door. Go inside. Satisfy her curiosity that Grandfather assuredly wasn't there.

*Meow.*

She jerked her hand away, strode to the front door and clumsily undid the locks, stumbling in her haste to get out of the house.

Busy with the tiller, Jones didn't notice her less-than-graceful exit, giving her a chance to study him. He'd removed his shirt and tossed it onto the porch. Sweat sheened on his back, rippling as he worked the tiller in a north/south line, amending the beds he'd already tilled. His skin was brown, a deep tan adding to the rich olive hue he came by naturally, and muscles defined the long bare expanse, disappearing into the sweat-soaked waistband of his shorts. Her breath coming more shallowly, she raised her gaze up again, to where his dark hair curled wetly against his neck.

She saw handsome men every day in New Orleans. She saw handsome men half-dressed and sweaty every day, and while she always appreciated them, she didn't grow short of breath looking at them. Her fingers didn't itch to touch them, to feel the heat radiating from them, to comb through their damp hair. For heaven's sake, she was a twenty-eight-year-old woman, not a fifteen-year-old girl.

Sudden silence made her realize he'd seen her and shut off the machine. She strolled down the steps, absently counting *one, two, three, four,* then stopped at the bottom. "Marvin?"

Removing the ear cups that protected his ears from the tiller's noise, he quirked one brow.

"Is that your name?"

"Nope. But I have an uncle Marvin."

"Leonard?"

"Nope. He's my cousin."

"Homer?"

Grinning, he shook his head. "That's my grandpa."

"You're kidding."

"Nope. And my other grandfather's name is Cleland. I come from more Joneses than a census taker could count. Name a name, and I've probably got a relative who answers to it." He wheeled the tiller off to one side, then swiped his face on a bandanna he pulled from his hip pocket. "What do you think?"

She walked out into the grass to get the full effect of the new beds. There was one on each side of the steps, blocky, their straight lines broken only by diamond points in the center of each bed. The freshly tilled earth smelled rich and lush, an intoxicating fragrance, like the first whiff of coffee early in the morning. Again, she felt a yearning to dig her hands into the soil, grind it into the knees of her jeans, cake it under her nails. Which would just earn her more disapproval from Grandmother.

"I like the points."

"Every bed had them originally, except in the shade garden, which really didn't have any beds at all. Things just grew kind of wild."

"When do the brick people come?"

His grin was way too charming to leave any female unaffected, whether she was fifteen or fifty-five. "You're looking at him."

"You're just a master of all trades, aren't you?"

"When you work with different tradesmen on every job, it helps to know the job yourself. You want to help?" When she arched her own brow, he said, "I saw the gleam in your eye when you saw the pansies, and then when you got your first whiff of soil. Miss Willa and Valerie might not like getting their hands dirty, but there's a gardener inside you."

She didn't bother telling him that any gleam in her eyes lately had been inspired by *him*. Her kiss earlier had gotten that message across clearly. "I'll go change."

She jogged up the steps and went inside, nudging

the door shut behind her. As if yanked from her hand, it slammed, echoing through the house, and a puff of cigar smoke billowed around her.

*Go away.*

For a moment, she froze, then remembered Jones just outside. Batting at the smoke, she started up the stairs, but the words echoed again as she reached the top and an extraordinarily icy patch of air. "You go away," she whispered with a glance toward Grandmother's closed door.

Inside her room she started to strip off her jeans, hesitated, then grabbed the clothes she wanted and stepped behind the changing screen in the corner. She didn't want to be ogled by any ghost, but especially a smelly, bossy one who was likely related to her.

She'd replaced jeans with comfortable cotton shorts and was unbuttoning her shirt when a squeak came from the other side of the screen. Part of her job at Martine's shop included cleaning glass display cases. She knew the sound of moisture on glass.

Sticking her head around the screen, she watched an unseen finger write on the mirror, the words appearing slowly.

*You may not live to regret the answers.*

"Are you *threatening* me?"

The first message faded, then what sounded like a sigh—and smelled of tobacco—shivered cold air through the room. "Go home. Forget that summer."

These words were as clear as her own, the voice as curt and ominous in death as it had been in life. Then, after a long pause, came another word, one she doubted he'd ever said in life, certainly not to the annoying granddaughter who'd disrupted his home for four months.

"Please."

Slowly she withdrew behind the screen again, though she was certain Grandfather was gone. She removed her shirt and tugged a T-shirt over her head. *Welcome to New Orleans,* it read over a picture of Jackson Square. *Now go home.* The words struck her as…ironic? Prophetic?

With flip-flops and a ballcap to shade her eyes, she returned to the front yard without incident.

Her part of the work was easy. Jones prepared the base for the brick retaining wall that would enclose the garden while she followed his directions. They talked about inconsequential things, the topics two new co-workers might discuss…or a couple on their first date.

And this—helping to build a brick wall, albeit minimally—was more fun than any first date she'd ever been on.

He explained to her that each row of bricks was called a course, and showed her how to be sure the courses were level, how to slather mortar onto the bricks and position each one. She even laid a few herself, using his gloves that were too big and were damp from his own hands, because Portland cement was harsh on the skin.

They were taking a break, sitting in the shade cast by a majestic live oak and drinking bottles of cold water that he'd retrieved from an ice chest in the pickup bed, and she was thinking how out of shape she was for physical labor, when the front door silently swung open. Ghost or Grandmother? she wondered, then Grandmother stepped out onto the porch. Her gaze flickered over Reece, her mouth tightening, then she took in the progress Jones had made.

"You'll be ready to plant soon."

"Yes, ma'am."

She looked again, then made eye contact with Reece. "Supper is in fifteen minutes. If you delay, the leftovers will be in the refrigerator, and you will clean up after yourself."

"Yes, ma'am," Reece echoed Jones. As the door closed, she wrapped her arms around her knees, resting her chin. "Do you suppose she cleans up after herself on Lois's days off?"

"I imagine not. Though she's probably very neat by nature."

"You'd think I'm some sort of slob, the way she acts, but I'm not. Except for the clothes I left on the floor when I changed, but that wasn't my fault." She told him about Grandfather's visit.

When she was done, he gazed thoughtfully into the distance. "Have you considered taking his advice?"

"And going home? No. I came here to find out what happened that summer."

"Sounds like he wants his family secrets to stay secret." Jones stretched out his legs, leaning back on his elbows, and studied her. "What's the worst case? You remember a little less of your childhood than most people do."

"I have nightmares."

"Take sleeping pills. See a therapist."

She scowled at him. "I *want* to know."

"There's a reason your brain blocked it out to start with. You couldn't handle it."

"I was thirteen. I can handle anything now."

He tilted his head to one side, studying her before quietly asking, "Are you sure? Have you considered all the possible reasons you blocked it? Maybe you were attacked that summer. Or molested. Maybe you witnessed something."

"Like what?" Her voice didn't sound like the voice of a woman who could handle anything, she noticed, and clamped her jaws shut.

Jones shrugged. "An attack on someone else. A death. A murder." Another shrug.

She swallowed hard, wanting to protest that none of those things could possibly have happened. Something that significant would stand out in her memory, not disappear into blackness. She would have remembered.

But that was the point. She couldn't *remember*.

And if the event *had* involved an attack, molestation or someone else's death, was she sure she *wanted* to?

Yes. Knowing was better than not knowing. She could always deal with knowing, with the help of time, friends and maybe a therapist. But not knowing…for fifteen years, not knowing had been the worst thing in her life.

Very quietly she repeated, "I *want* to know."

Jones understood. Hell, he felt the same way about Glen. He needed to know what had happened to his brother. But he couldn't help but think he was better able to handle his own nightmare than Reece was hers. Which didn't make any sense. Neither of them had family to turn to for support, but at least she had a couple of best friends. He had a lot of buddies, but no one that close. And though she might not look it, she was tough. Coming back here proved it.

They worked until the sun was low in the sky. As they cleaned up, he caught her grimacing with the discomfort of muscles unaccustomed to his kind of work.

"You want to take a shower and ride into town with me for a burger?"

That wasn't at all what he wanted to offer, he realized the instant she turned toward him. The shower part, okay. They were both caked with sweat, dirt and cement dust, and he knew from long experience that he smelled about as bad as he looked.

But he didn't want to go into town. He didn't want a burger. He didn't even want to get dressed after the shower. And he wanted to take that together.

She removed the ballcap and ran her fingers through her damp hair. "I suppose I should eat whatever Lois prepared for Grandmother." A light flickered on, the dim illumination of a pole-mounted lamp above the driveway. She looked up, appearing to listen to its hum for a moment, then smiled. "I'll meet you on the patio as soon as I'm clean."

He watched her go into the house, and continued to watch for a while before a breeze stirred that brought his attention back. He gave the area around him an exasperated look. "If ol' Arthur can hang around and pass on messages, why can't you, Glen?"

There was no answer, no sight or sound out of place.

"You always did like to make me work for stuff." Giving a whistle for Mick, he headed for the cottage. The dog joined him from the spot where he'd been sleeping on the patio, trotted inside the house and climbed onto the sofa, settling in comfortably.

Jones was quick at showering and dressing. With five brothers and sisters, he'd had to be. He put out fresh water and food for the dog, then walked to the door. Mick followed him with a mournful whine. Jones told him no, told him that he was just taking Reece out for a burger. Whether it was the mention of Reece or the burger that excited the mutt, he wasn't sure, but somehow when he locked up and walked back to the house, the dog was beside him.

The only lights visible in the big house came from the downstairs hallway and Reece's front upstairs bedroom. Either Miss Willa's room was on the other side of the house, or she went to bed awfully early.

Before he reached the table that was his destination, the side door opened and Reece came out. She was dressed like him—jeans, T-shirt—and her hair, like his, was still damp. If she'd put on makeup, he couldn't tell—which was the point of makeup, his older sister had once told him. Though both his sisters had worn a lot of it, and his nieces, if he had any, had likely dipped into their mothers' cosmetics—and fashion style—about the time they started kindergarten.

One of the traditions he'd been happy to leave behind.

"Is your grandmother settled for the night?"

"She's in her room with the door closed. One of the first lessons I learned here was that meant leave her alone." Her smile was faint. "I left a note for her."

For the first time in Jones's memory, Mick willingly gave up the front passenger seat for someone else, jumping over the console to the rear seat, then sitting with his chin on the seat's back so Reece could scratch him. He thought of their conversation about relationships, when he'd silently listed what she was looking for: *loving her dogs unconditionally.*

He had to admit, he was pretty much a sucker for someone who treated Mick the way she did.

Instead of a hamburger joint, they wound up at a table on a small brick patio outside Ellie's Deli, where a friendly waitress named Gina supplied Mick with a chew toy and a bowl of water. She asked for their drinks, and Jones ordered a beer, Reece iced tea. When Gina returned with the drinks and took their dinner orders—they both got burgers, after all—he picked up the icy bottle and studied it a moment.

All afternoon he'd been wondering when to tell her what he'd learned from Mark. Well, not all afternoon, he corrected himself as he watched her lay the straw aside and lift the glass of tea to her lips, drinking long and slow. He'd spent a good part of it wondering when they would get to finish that kiss, because it wasn't done, not by a long shot.

But the conversation with Mark had been in the back of his mind, stewing there behind the lust and need. It wouldn't give her all the answers she wanted, and it was only gossip stirred by someone with a dislike for the subject, but Reece had a right to hear it. It was up to her what to do with it.

He gestured with his beer bottle to her iced tea. "Do you drink?"

"Not really."

"Is that on moral, religious or medical grounds?"

She shook her head. "My parents drank wine every evening and always celebrated special events with champagne. Grandmother liked wine with meals, too, while Grandfather drank good ol' Kentucky bourbon. The evening glasses of wine stopped for Valerie after my dad died. I guess it reminded her too much of him, that it was something they'd shared. I tried booze a few times, as most kids do in their teens, but I never liked the taste of it."

Jones watched a black Charger cruise past, then pull into the last parking space before River Road. Tommy Maricci got out, and Jones's nerves tightened. *I'll be in touch,* Maricci had told him. Was that his reason for stopping?

The detective walked up the sidewalk, giving them a polite nod as he climbed the steps and went inside. Through the open screen door, Jones saw him greet a pretty blonde with a kiss, then take a dark-haired child from her and give him a hug and a tickle. He was just meeting his wife for dinner. He had no news about Glen.

Jones breathed and refocused on Reece. "I ran into Mark again this afternoon. After we left the tire store."

"Lucky you. Trying to bribe you to leave Copper Lake?"

"No. He, uh, mentioned your mother—how she suddenly came back that summer and took you away. He said it was unexpected. She blew in and blew out with you in tow."

Her expression was thoughtful. "Did he say where she'd been?"

"He'd heard the same explanations you had. But, uh, his mother thought that your mother might have, uh, been...well, in rehab during that time." There. He'd said it. It had been harder than telling a client he was looking at a six-figure overrun. But with Lori keeping a tight control on the budgets, major overruns were almost always the clients' fault, and that was strictly business. He didn't get emotionally attached to clients.

And he was getting emotionally attached to Reece.

Reece's expression shifted—surprise? Understanding? Acceptance? "Rehab... That would explain..."

A lot. Why Valerie had given Reece's care totally over to strangers. Why she'd stopped having those evening glasses of wine. Why she refused to discuss the subject with her daughter all these years later.

"Rehab," she repeated. "She was so distraught about Daddy. You see families on TV, when a loved one dies, and they're sad but composed, dry-eyed, coping. That was Grandmother. She was stoic, like a proper Howard, but not Valerie. She sobbed for days. She was so fragile. The doctor had to sedate her after the ashes-scattering service in Colorado, and she didn't even get out of bed for a week after the memorial service here. She rarely came out of her room for more than a few minutes, and when she did, she was a mess. Rehab makes sense." She nodded slowly as if confirming it to herself.

He reached for her hand, cold and stiff, and folded his fingers around it. "Which means she didn't abandon you. Not intentionally."

She didn't say anything to that—just gazed into the distance—but her fingers tightened just a bit around his. Did hearing her aunt's gossip offer any comfort? Or was abandonment abandonment, no matter what the reason?

She didn't look as if she'd reached a decision on that when Gina brought their food. Squeezing his hand again, she murmured, "Thank you," before sliding her fingers loose and unrolling the linen napkin next to her plate. She didn't say anything else until they were halfway through their meal. "What kind of mother was your mom, other than fertile?"

"Fertility runs in the family. That's why Big Dan taught us boys to never even go near a female without condoms at hand." He took a bite of hamburger and chewed it while his mind wandered across the state line into South Carolina, to the big house just off Highway 25. They'd built the house when he was fourteen, but he'd never gotten to live in it. Tradition required a new house remain empty for a year before the family could move in, and by the end of that year, he'd been gone.

His mother had been proud of the fancy house, the new cars, the jewelry, of her husband and her children. She'd protected them fiercely, as fiercely as she'd protected the family traditions. He figured Big Dan would come closer to forgiving him than his mother ever would.

"She was a typical mother. She loved us even when we were getting on her last nerve. She wanted the same kind of life for us that she and our father had. We heard a lot of 'Wait till your father gets home,' but she was really the one who put the fear of God in us."

"And yet you walked away from that. What did you want that you couldn't get there?"

"Freedom."

"Was it worth it?" She smiled faintly. "Life is meant to be lived with family. Not just parents and grandparents and stepparents, but siblings, cousins, aunts and uncles, the more, the merrier. You gave all that up. Was it worth it?"

"Yes." He didn't hesitate over the answer, nor was he embarrassed by it, though some part of him felt as if he should be when she'd wanted a family and been denied a real one for more than half her life.

"Freedom to do what?"

"Freedom to *not* do," he replied. Finished with his meal, he leaned back in the chair. The streetlights were buzzing, voices sounded through the windows and on the sidewalks, and music came from a restaurant across the street. If the night were ten degrees warmer—and the conversation more casual—it would be the most comfortable he'd been in a while.

"My family had certain expectations for me. They couldn't accept that I wanted something more."

"What expectations?"

Jones sighed. He'd told Detective Maricci the truth. He could tell Reece. Hell, she might not have a clue who or what the Travelers were—their reputation, their activities. But he could guarantee Miss Willa knew, as surely as Maricci had.

"My family is very insular. My brothers and I were raised to follow in our father's and grandfathers' footsteps. My sisters' lives would be just like our mother's and grandmothers'. We'd be in the same business, live in the same community, teach our children the same values."

"Sounds like a religious cult," she said cautiously.

He grinned. Not a cult, but a clan. A very close-knit, like-minded, strict-living clan. "No, just plain ol' Catholics. I love my family. They're not bad people. They're just very set in their ways, and I wanted something different."

"And they can't forgive you for that?"

"I disappointed them. They don't forgive easily."

"Sounds like you shocked the socks off them." She sighed heavily, too. "Welcome to the club. Grandfather didn't know the meaning of the word *forgive,* and Grandmother might do it, but she never forgets. I think she'd find it easier if I said I was sorry for missing his funeral, but I'm not. I just couldn't face it."

"A reasonable person wouldn't expect you to." Even if the old man had never laid a hand on her—and God, Jones hoped that was true—the fact remained that Arthur had terrified and traumatized a kid. The child could be forgiven for the state of their relationship. The supposedly mature, responsible adult couldn't.

Reece laughed at his comment. "You expect Grandmother to be reasonable? She doesn't have to. She's a Howard, you know."

"So are you."

Her leftover smile faded. "Only in name, Jones. Only in name."

When Jones excused himself to go inside the restaurant, Mick moved to Reece's side, placing his head where she could easily rub the favored spot between his ears. The action was repetitive, soothing, and allowed her to let her thoughts wander.

Valerie an alcoholic. Yes, that fit. If she closed her eyes and looked back in time, she had vague images of her mother, totally undone, eyes puffy, face swollen, fingers clenching tightly a tall, clear bottle. She'd raged at everyone who ventured near—Reece, Grandmother, the housekeeper. The best Reece could remember, Grandfather hadn't tried to approach her, though he had retrieved that bottle from her room a time or two.

She could call Valerie and ask, but she would likely get the same response she'd always gotten: *Really, Clarice. The past is past.* And then she would change the subject to something inane and totally inconsequential.

Better that she ask Grandmother. It was less personal with her, so she was more likely to answer. Though only if she wanted to.

Movement near the screen door caught her eye, and she saw Jones talking to a muscular dark-haired guy. The guy was holding a child, two, maybe three years old. With its shaggy hair, jeans and a T-shirt, she couldn't tell whether it was a boy or girl.

Their conversation appeared serious until the child

broke in. Whatever he said made Jones grin and tickle his tummy, which made the kid squeal with laughter.

The simple action touched something inside Reece.

After a moment, Jones returned to the table. "I paid the check while I was inside. Ready to go?"

Mick leaped to his feet. Like with her dogs, *go* was a magic word. No matter how much Bubba, Louie and Eddie loved where they were, they were always thrilled to *go* somewhere else.

She stood, and Jones automatically reached for her hand. She naturally let him take it. It felt normal. Good. And just the mere presence of him felt promising.

She'd been hopeful in the beginning with other men, she reminded herself. Not every new relationship came with that sense of promise, potential, future, but a few had, and look what had happened: every one had ended. And those were with guys who lived in the same part of the country she did, never mind the same city.

This thing with Jones wasn't likely to be any different, even if he was open to the idea of a long-distance relationship.

A CD played quietly on the stereo on the drive home, classic rock, hits from a band that had peaked before either of them had been born. It was one of her favorites.

When they reached Fair Winds, he entered the code and the gate swung slowly open. With little moon and too much shadow, the place looked eerie—nothing new there. But she didn't feel the eeriness quite as sharply as she normally would have. Too bad she couldn't just attach herself to Jones and hold on to that safe feeling the whole time she was here.

Mists swirled in the shadows as they drove along the drive, despite the fact that the air was calm, and awareness hummed along her veins, as surely as if their voices were in her ears. It was just plain creepy, even if she *was* safe with Jones.

He parked beside the cottage, shut off the engine and looked at her. "Want to make out while we're here?"

With a laugh, she considered the broad console between them. "I don't think this truck is made for making out. That's a long way to lean."

"Or you could just come over here and sit on my lap." He tilted the steering wheel up and out of away, then grinned as he offered her a hand.

Making out was good. She'd never had any trouble handling that. She climbed across the console, wriggling and twisting to get comfortable, and drawing a grunt from him in the process. Once she was settled, he didn't kiss her right away, though. Instead, with one arm around her shoulders, he touched her face with his free hand. "You're a beautiful woman, Clarice. I always thought…"

When he fell silent, she prodded him to go on. "Thought what?"

He seemed lost for a moment, then his mouth quirked. "The girl my mother picked out for me to marry was a redhead with watery blue eyes, but I always had a weakness for brown-eyed blondes."

"Your mother picked out a bride for you?" she echoed. "Just how old were you when you left home?"

"Fifteen."

Her eyes widened. "You were just a kid."

"So were you back then," he retorted. "We've both grown up."

There was no denying that, not sitting the way they were, her on his lap and his fingertips just grazing the side of her breast. "So…what? She was your mother's best friend's daughter and they thought 'wouldn't it be great if our kids got married'?" Her voice hitched as those feathery little caresses continued.

"Something like that." There was some emotion in his voice, too—dark, deep, sending tiny shivers along her arms. But he didn't say anything more because he was kissing her, sweet nibbling tastes, starting with her forehead and working his way to the corner of her mouth, then the bottom lip, then the bow in the center.

She opened her mouth and his tongue dipped inside, and something deep in her dissolved. This was good. Promising. Full of potential and future.

They kissed leisurely, touched slowly, as if they had the entire rest of their lives to do nothing but explore each other. It was sweet and lazy, and the heat built slowly. They took it easy, a new experience for Reece with first-time sex. He wanted to get her clothes off—she could feel that tension thrumming through his body and into hers, could feel the erection swelling against her hip—but there was no rush. They could take the time to do it right.

In the backseat, Mick gave a little whine, then exploded in a frenzy of barking, hitting the seat with such force in an attempt to get out of the driver's window that it jarred Reece and Jones apart. "Hey," Jones started to complain, but he recognized before she did that this wasn't routine, want-out-of-the-truck barking. His muscles tightening, Jones twisted beneath her to look off to the east for the source of Mick's sudden alert.

By the time Jones started to lift her away, Reece was already scrambling onto the console. "There's a light in that shed," he said quietly. "It wasn't there when we pulled in. I would have noticed it. You stay here—"

"Like hell." When he slid out the open door, she was right behind him. He scowled at her, but Mick bounding out of the truck, hair on end, and racing toward the shed claimed his attention.

The shed was fifty feet past the garage, an identical structure with an overhead door and a smaller side door. The light shone through the panes of glass in the side door and leaked under the front one. Jones was right, she thought as she matched her strides to his. The light gleamed in the darkness; they would have noticed it when they'd come home.

Mick reached the shed far ahead of them and ran from door to door, quivering, snarling, nose to the ground searching for scent. Jones peered through the door glass, but it was covered—painted white, Reece abruptly recalled. To let light in and keep nosy looks out.

He silently tried the knob, but it was locked. Moving to the overhead door, he twisted the handle to unlock it, gave her a steady look until she backed away a few feet, then heaved it open.

The long-unused mechanism shrieked, and Reece clapped her hands over her ears, trying to ignore the queasiness in her stomach and the goose bumps popping up everywhere.

A naked bulb dangled overhead, its pull-chain swaying slightly, showing and shadowing the only items in the building: Grandfather's old truck, two shovels leaning against one wall and a pile of canvas tarps neatly folded on a rough-built shelf. Another tarp was hung to dry over the side wall of the pickup bed, an aged dark stain making it stiff where it should have draped.

Jones went into the shed, looking around the truck,

under it, inside the cab. There was no place for anyone to hide.

No place for Reece to hide.

*Oh, God, what have I done?* The words were years old, the tone so harsh and horrified that she couldn't recognize it.

And the response, too quiet to hear.

The heat of that long-ago August afternoon beat down on her as she stiffened in place, staring through the open door. Such anger, evil and hate—such utter coldness—emanated from the space.

She choked back a cry as she stumbled back a step, terror flooding into her very bones, drawing their attention to her.

*Get back in the house!*

And the tiny voice inside her, echoing nearly as loud as Grandfather's roar: *Run, run, run!*

Heart thudding, vision blurring, she spun around and dashed away. Dimly she heard a dog bark, a man shout, but she didn't slow. Her arms swung, her legs pumping, her strides closing the distance, but, God, not fast enough. He was chasing her—Grandfather? Mark? He was stronger, faster, and she was too slow, too clumsy. Her feet slid in the gravel, and she tripped over a hank of grass when she veered off the road.

He caught her, arms wrapping around her, holding her close. His breathing was loud in her ears, his voice unfamiliar as he murmured, "It's okay, Reece, it's okay. Just an old memory. It can't hurt you. They can't hurt you. It's just you and me and Mick. You're safe."

She inhaled sharply, intending to scream, but the scents caught in her nose: soap, shampoo, cologne, dog. She knew those scents. She trusted them.

Jones. Mick.

Pivoting, she wrapped her arms around his neck and held on as if only he could chase away the fear, the ghosts, the memories. Only he could make her feel safe.

She held on for dear life.

## Chapter 9

Silently cursing, Jones scooped her into his arms, choking at the strength with which she gripped his neck, and walked to the cottage with long strides. What the hell had happened? Had the mere sight of the old truck brought that memory of her grandfather and Mark back to vivid life? Judging by the sheer panic in her eyes, he'd say yes. She hadn't been merely remembering. She'd been living it again.

Balancing her on one hip and against the door frame, he got the front door open and carried her to the couch. She was trembling, making a terrible keening sound that set his nerves on edge. It worried Mick, too, who stood beside the couch for only a moment before trotting back to the screen door to peer out, then trotted back to the couch. On guard, like a good dog.

Jones couldn't get her to let go long enough to set her down, so he sat instead, settling her on his lap. He'd never dealt with a hysterical woman before. He didn't know what to say or do, so he held her, stroked her, murmured promises to her. *It's all right. You're safe. I won't let them hurt you.*

He hoped he wasn't lying.

After a time, the keening stopped. Traditionally, he knew, it was a mourning for the dead. Was it purely an emotional response? Or had she witnessed a death? A murder. Glen's murder.

The shudders slowed, losing their violence, fading into occasional tremors before disappearing entirely. She lay limp in his arms, probably exhausted by the shock, and her voice, when she spoke, was weak. "The stain on that tarp, it's blood. I'm sure of it. I smelled it."

Glen's blood? Would it be possible to prove after all these years? Jones knew science as it pertained to plants, not people. But Maricci would know. He would know where to send it, and where Jones could give a sample if DNA was retrieved to see if it matched.

His muscles ached to set Reece aside and go now: get the tarp, jump in his truck, call Maricci on the way into town. But it was late, and he couldn't just set Reece aside. She needed him. The tarp had survived this long. It would keep until tomorrow.

He could put off knowing for absolute sure that Glen was dead for a little while longer. Though he felt it in his bones, as long as he didn't have definitive proof, some part of him could still hope…

"Whose blood?" he asked softly.

Staring into the distance, she shook her head.

"What did you see, Reece?"

"The same thing," she said dully. "Grandfather, Mark, the truck. It was August. So hot, so humid. There was such threat in his voice. I'd only seen him like that once before, when I..."

The thought seemed to strike them both at the same time. When she'd repeated the memory to him earlier, she'd said, *He was angrier than I'd ever seen him.*

Her gaze met his. "One day he caught me digging in the yard, and he was livid. He grabbed my shoulders and lifted me right off the ground and said, 'Do you know what happens to little girls who poke around where they don't belong?' Then he set me down and dragged me to the front door, where he bent down right in my face. He said, 'If you ever tell anyone...' And I didn't wait for him to finish. I ran inside and straight to Grandmother's study. I didn't say a word to anyone, but every day I looked at the bruises he'd left, then stayed as close as I could to Grandmother or the housekeeper, until they got tired of it and made me go outside."

Jones grimly stared at her. "Were you digging in the front yard? Where the garden used to be?"

She nodded.

Arthur Howard may have been a good man as far as his family, excluding Reece's father, was concerned, but he'd definitely had a secret to keep. His destruction of the gardens, his fury at Reece for digging there, his messages from the grave for her to get out...

Could that secret be Glen's body? Even though Mark said he'd never told his grandfather about Jones and Glen, that didn't mean the old man hadn't discovered Glen on his own. Hell, they'd seen him in the woods several times, striding about like a king surveying his kingdom. He'd felt so secure on his property that he'd never seemed the slightest bit aware that there were trespassers who watched him from the cover of low growth or sturdy tree branches.

And Glen had been worried about Reece. He'd intended to move his camp off Howard property, but he would have sneaked back close to the house to watch for her. If Arthur had caught him…

Had the old man really been violent enough to kill a trespasser rather than chase him away or call the sheriff? He'd deliberately, cruelly traumatized his own granddaughter. He'd had a cold, uncaring side, along with the strong sense of entitlement that came from being a Howard in a place where that meant everything. He'd been taught he could do what he wanted and that money, power and the family name would protect him.

What was it Russ Calloway's grandmother had said about him? That she believed Arthur had kept leasing that land where Glen's backpack was found because *he wanted as much land between him and the world as he could get.* Between his secrets and the world.

His head starting to throb, Jones shifted underneath Reece until they were both lying on the couch, face-to-face in the narrow space. "Why were you digging in the yard?"

"I don't know." She pushed back to give him an inch or two more of space, and he took it, moving until their bodies were snugly pressed together again. Her hand rested on his rib cage, her knee between his. "When I left here that summer, I dug a lot. I planted garden beds everywhere Valerie would let me. I also had nightmares, a new fear of deep water and counted."

"Counted what?"

"Steps. You know, when I walk. One, two, three, but only up to thirty-eight. Not all the time, but when I'm anxious or my mind's wandering or I'm thinking about that summer." She flushed. "It used to drive Valerie crazy because I did it out loud, so I learned to keep quiet, and she thought I stopped. Now my best friends, Evie and Martine, are the only ones who know."

"And me." It touched him that she trusted him with the secret. Shouldn't he trust her with his? At least he could explain the reason behind her fear of water, and maybe some prodding would help unleash other memories.

"Reece—"

She laid her fingers over his mouth. "No. That sounds like the start to more serious conversation, and I can't do it anymore tonight. Make me laugh, Jones. Make me feel good. Make me forget everything else in the world but you and me."

He pushed her fingers aside after pressing a kiss to them. "I don't know—"

She did laugh, not wholeheartedly but a little chuckle of amusement. "Oh, you do know. Like you were doing—*we* were doing—in the truck before Mick interrupted. Make me forget, Jones. Just for tonight."

He wanted to tell her no, this wasn't the right time, certainly not the right reason, but she looked so vulnerable and her hand was under his shirt, spreading heat across his skin, and they'd already been headed this way before the latest interference. He'd already wanted her, and she'd already wanted him, and they could make it the right time and the right reason. They could laugh together, feel good together, forget together...

And, tomorrow or the next day or next week, they could remember together.

They could do damn near anything together.

Reece awakened sometime in the night with a sense of well-being she hadn't experienced since the day she'd driven out of New Orleans. It wasn't a nightmare that had roused her—a happy exception—but the simple need to change positions, to pull her covers a little tighter, then go back to sleep. Good rest came rarely. She would take advantage of it.

The instant she shifted her weight to roll over, something else in the room shifted, too. For just an instant there was complete silence, sound conspicuous due to its absence, then the noise she easily identified as Mick's breathing started again, slow and easy.

For a moment she considered why Mick was in her room, but realized the opposite was true from the heat radiating behind her. Jones, his breathing as slow and easy as Mick's. She turned carefully, trying not to disturb him, and settled onto the pillow again, watching him in the thin light. She couldn't really make out anything—the suggestion of a nose, the darker slash of eyebrow, the rest too shadowy—but she didn't need to see to picture him. Memories of him would stay with her forever. The way he'd run after her, the way he'd held her, the way he'd soothed her, the way he'd made love to her, the way he'd fallen asleep holding her, making her feel…

Good. She felt good. Because of him, she would survive this visit. She might return home without all the answers she'd been seeking, but she would be better for the things she'd learned.

Even if one of those things was that her grandfather was a murderer.

A chill passed through her, and at the foot of the bed, Mick lifted his head with a whine. He stood, stretched all over, then hopped off the bed and trotted to the door. There he looked back as if to make sure she was following, then went into the living room. A moment later, he nosed the front door.

Homesick for her own dogs, she slipped from the bed, located her clothes and set them on the night table, then pulled on Jones's T-shirt and padded after Mick. She let him out into the cool night, hugging her arms to her chest, and watched as he sniffed around the truck, then lifted his leg at the corner of the porch.

The shed down the road drew her gaze. The light was off, the door closed. Jones had gone to lock it up after they'd made love the first time, and he'd returned looking puzzled. She'd known without asking that the shed had been shut up by the same whoever—whatever—had lit it up for them to find, and without the terrible screech of the overhead door.

Mist swirled, though the humidity was no higher tonight than usual, and she wondered if those ethereal shapes drifting about with purpose were spirits. A distant wail from the direction of the woods that sounded faintly like tears convinced her she didn't want to know.

Mick's nails clicked across the wooden porch, his fur brushing her legs as he eased inside. She was happy to close and lock the door behind him.

Dim light fell in a wedge from the kitchen into the living room. Reece paused midstep, certain she hadn't turned on the bulb over the sink. She had assumed the cottage was haunt-free—she'd never heard of anything happening there. But Jones had told her—as Evie had, as Martine had—that ghosts attached to places *or* people. Was Grandfather's ghost attaching to her, or was she mistaken in attributing all her otherworldly experiences to just one soul?

The light arrowed in on a small walnut table at the

end of the sofa, just strong enough to give the gilt lettering of its title a bit of gleam. *Southern Aristocracy.*

She was more than certain she hadn't brought the book to the cottage.

Restlessly she picked up the book, her nose wrinkling at the musty smell, and flipped through the pages. The first time she found nothing. The second time, the pages of the middle third opened to reveal a piece of thick ivory linen writing paper.

*He isn't what he seems.*

After reading the single line a half-dozen times, she shifted her gaze to the bedroom door. Was Jones the *he* Grandfather meant? As if she would trust his opinion on anything. He'd terrorized her for half her life. Even dead, he was still trying to frighten her away, not only from Fair Winds but now from the only person who'd made any effort to help her. The only person she'd felt something...*real* with in years.

*But what do you really know about him?*

She couldn't tell whether the voice echoing in her head was her own or Grandfather's or, hell, even someone else's, and she flushed hot with guilt. She knew enough.

*His own family wants nothing to do with him.*

"Oh, please." Slamming the book shut, she set it back on the table. "Like that makes him the bad guy? My father wanted nothing to do with you, and that was *your* fault. *I* wanted nothing to do with you, and that was your fault, too."

Silence met her whisper, and after a moment of it, she was sure she was alone again. She went into the bedroom, where Mick was already snoozing again on a blanket folded under the window and Jones was sprawled across most of the bed, covers down to his waist.

*He isn't what he seems,* the note echoed.

She thought of him, of the way they'd connected, of the way he'd cared for her. Taken care of and with her. No one had done that in so very long.

Why shouldn't she trust him? He had nothing to gain from a relationship with her, and she had nothing to risk besides her heart. Sometimes that was a risk worth taking.

Slipping out of the shirt, she climbed into bed. As she snuggled close, Jones wrapped his arm around her waist, left a sleepy kiss on her neck and settled her in with a soft, contented, "Umm."

Definitely worth a risk.

She dozed a few more hours, and when she awakened again, the quality of the darkness had changed. It was dawn, everything quiet outside, everything mostly quiet in, but she wasn't the only one awake. Opening her eyes, she found Jones lying on his side, watching her, his expression deep and intense.

"If you don't want Miss Willa to know you spent the night here, you'd better go now." His voice was a rumble in the shadows, husky, comforting.

"I don't care if she knows, though it may be easier for you if I go now."

"I don't care if she knows, either." After a moment, he raised one hand to stroke her hair back. "Are you okay?"

"You mean, have I adjusted to the fact that my grandfather was probably a murderer?" She tried to smile, but it came out more of a grimace. "Before I even understood what evil was, I sensed he was bad. Valerie said I let Daddy prejudice me against him. Well, yeah.

My father loved everybody, but he could hardly bear to look at my grandfather. He only brought us here when the pressure from Valerie and Grandmother got too much for him, and he always kept our visits short."

She paused, a detail becoming clear that she'd long forgotten. "He never left me alone when we were here. Whatever I did—fish, explore, read—he did it with me. Always. Do you think he *knew* that his father had killed someone and did nothing about it besides keep us far away?"

"No." Jones didn't hesitate. "You said he was a good guy. He probably just suspected there was something *off* about your grandfather. If he'd known the truth, he would have gone to the authorities, even if they were family, even if he wanted to protect his mother. That's what good guys do."

Nodding, she relaxed against the pillow again. Daddy *had* been good. He was the one everyone turned to for help, the one who couldn't drive past a car broken down on the side of the road without offering assistance, the one who mentored troubled kids and mowed yards for neighbors who couldn't do it themselves and volunteered at the soup kitchen. It wasn't in him to sit back and do nothing.

"The man I was talking to at dinner last night, the one with the kid, he's a detective in Copper Lake. I'd like to show him the tarp—see if there's a chance of proving the stain is blood, maybe proving whose it is."

She swallowed hard. She didn't know whether they could legally turn it over to the authorities, but Grandfather was dead; he couldn't be taken to trial. And if it was blood, if the victim could be identified, didn't his family deserve to know?

"All right," she murmured. "But maybe I should call

your detective friend. Maybe you should stay out of it. It's no big deal if Grandmother throws me out."

His grin was faint. "It's no big deal if she fires me, either. In fact, if she did, there are some damn fine gardens in New Orleans that I've been meaning to visit."

The tightness in her chest eased a bit. He wanted to see her after they left here. She wasn't just an on-site diversion.

"I'll call Maricci," he said.

"If he needs to come out here and you want me to keep Grandmother occupied, just let me know." Pushing back the sheet, she swung her legs over the side of the bed and shimmied into her panties. Her shirt came next—had she not worn a bra or just hadn't found it?— then her jeans. She was zipping up when tires crunched on the gravel outside. She glanced out the window though the driveway wasn't visible. The faint "Goodbye" drifting on the still air identified the arrival as the housekeeper, calling to her driver before closing the door.

Reece reached the bedroom door before turning back. "You'd go all the way to New Orleans just to see some gardens?"

"Maybe. But I'd definitely go to see you."

She grinned, waved and hustled across the living room, grabbing the book from the end table on her way. As she clenched it in one arm, she swore she could actually *feel* the warning note inside, drumming. *He isn't what he seems, he isn't what he seems.*

*He is,* she firmly argued. She believed that. She trusted him. *Trusted,* she who always had issues with trust.

She returned to the house, changed clothes and had breakfast—coffee, toast and an orange—on the front porch. Grandmother had stuck her head out when she finished her own meal for a stern hello, then retreated back inside to do whatever it was that filled her days.

When Reece's cell phone rang, it startled her. She carried it with her from habit, but this was the first call she'd gotten since leaving New Orleans. Evie's voice sounded cheery and energetic.

"No frantic calls saying, 'I need you!' so I'm guessing everything's going…well, if not great, then tolerably. How is your grandmother?"

"She's fine."

"And the ghosts?"

"They're in fine form, too."

Evie's tone grew more serious. "And you?"

Reece gazed across the lawn toward the river. Back when the gardens were magnificent, the grounds between fence and river had been maintained, too, so it was visible from the porch. Now scrub blocked all but the briefest views. "I'm okay. I've remembered a few things, got an answer or two. My cousin, Mark, lives in town, and he doesn't have horns and a pitchfork after all. Grandmother's as warm and fuzzy as ever. And…"

"And…?"

Reece drew her feet into the cushioned seat and said softly, "There's a guy here. His name is Jones, and he's doing a project for Grandmother." Though, as far as she knew, no contract had been signed yet.

"I take it he's gorgeous and wickedly sexy."

"He is."

"Do you remember him?"

"No. He lives in Kentucky. He's just here working."

"Oh, of course. Tell Sister Evie more. Was last night incredible?"

Reece grinned. Sometimes there were disadvantages

to having a psychic for a best friend. It was hard to keep secrets. But considering that half her life had been about secrets, maybe that was a good thing. "It was."

"Tell me the best thing about him."

Evie had made the request before, regarding other relationships Reece had gotten into—and, always, out of. Usually her answers were glib or average: *He's funny. He has great taste. He has great abs. He's gone.*

This time she answered earnestly. "I trust him."

After a moment of utter silence, Evie murmured, "Wow."

That was another thing about having a psychic for a best friend: it was hard to surprise her. But Reece had managed.

"Wow," Evie repeated. "I knew you should, but I didn't think *you* would know you should. Not yet. He's a good guy, Reece. In spite of everything else, trust that. Believe that."

Reece's fingers tightened. "I do," she answered automatically, then just as quickly asked, "In spite of what else?"

In the background came a shriek so shrill that Reece tilted the cell a few inches from her ear. "*Mama!* Isabella broke my car!" Jackson shouted over the wail.

"Isabella! Jackson! I'll have to talk to you later, Reece, okay? If you need me—" The decibels surrounding her spiked, making her sigh almost indistinguishable. "Really, think about needing me, will you? Love you."

"Love you, too." Reece disconnected, torn by the conversation. She was glad to hear Evie's endorsement of Jones, and always glad to have her friend agree with her assessment of someone. But what had she meant by *in spite of everything?* Being estranged from his family? Probably having to do some tough things to get by when he was just fifteen and on his own?

"'Love you, too,' hmm? I hope that was Valerie or Evie or Martine." Jones didn't bother with the center steps but climbed onto the porch at the end, his calf muscles flexing. His khaki shorts and T-shirt were both well-worn, as were the running shoes that looked as if they could walk on their own. He'd shaved the stubble from his chin, but had combed his hair with his fingers.

He looked incredible.

"Valerie and I aren't exactly the endearment type. That was Evie. She said you're a good guy."

His brows arched as he crouched in front of her, a post at his back. "How would she know— Oh, yeah, she's the one with the gift." The surprise settled into a grin that warmed her from the inside out. "She's right. I am a good guy."

"Do you want me to stroke your ego by agreeing?"

"I'd rather you stroke..." He broke off, and a dull tinge flushed his cheeks. "Sorry. I didn't mean to say that out loud."

She laughed. Laughter was such a rare thing around Fair Winds that she was half surprised the spirits hadn't come flying to see what was going on.

"I talked to Maricci. He's on his way out. If you don't mind distracting Miss Willa... I somehow don't think she's going to give him permission to poke around, especially if she has any clue what Arthur did."

That was another thought that had niggled at Reece since last night. She'd believed Jones's assurances that her father would have taken action if he'd known, but what about Grandmother? She'd been married to the man for more than fifty years. Could she really not have known what he was capable of? Or could he have been that good at fooling people?

Grandmother only acknowledged what she wanted to know, and Grandfather had only shown what he wanted to show. She had to live—and he'd had to die—with the choices they'd made. Their actions, or inactions, were their responsibilities.

"I can always ask her questions about family history. Better yet, we can have the conversation we haven't quite managed yet." She uncurled her legs, and Jones stood, offering her a hand up. His fingers gripped hers a minute longer than necessary, sending heat and assurance and strength her way. *A good guy.* She had a weakness for truly good guys.

When he released her hand, she gathered her dishes and went inside, taking one last look at him for encouragement.

A hum came from the door to Grandfather's study, reminding her of angry bees. Traveling the length of the hall, she passed through a couple of cold spots and steadfastly ignored creaking and rustling from the rooms she passed. Grandmother was in her study, a thick sheaf of papers on the desk in front of her. Reece waited to be acknowledged, which she got with a brief, dry look.

"I would like to talk to you if you have time."

Grandmother made an impatient gesture. "Seat yourself."

"Not here. In the salon." The driveway ran twenty feet from the study windows. There was no way Grandmother would miss a stranger's arrival there.

"Why the salon?"

"Because it's a lovely room that's rarely been used in the last century." In her limited experience, it seemed everyone had had their favorite places: Grandmother and Grandfather their studies, Valerie her bedroom, Mark wherever Grandfather was, Dad wherever Reece was and Reece outside. The only place they'd gathered as a family was at the dinner table.

Grandmother looked as if she might refuse—she was so accustomed to doing that—but instead she rose and led the way down the halls to the salon. "Every single piece in here came from distant lands. That chandelier is from France, those tables from India, the vases from China. The rugs are Persian, the lace is from Brussels, that glasswork from Murano. Captain Howard never made a voyage that he failed to bring home some treasure for the house he intended to build."

Reece seated herself in an uncomfortable chair that looked as if it might have come from France, as well, and immediately asked her first question. "What went wrong that my father left this house intending never to return?"

Grandmother's posture stiffened even more than its usual boardlike state. "He fell in love with your mother."

"People fall in love and move away from home all the time and still go back for summer visits, holidays, birthdays."

"Your father came back."

"How often in the sixteen years he was away? Twice? Three times? And he couldn't even speak to Grandfather when he was here."

Grandmother's scowl was stern, her gaze sharply disapproving, and would have made adolescent Reece quake and flee. Not this time. "Elliott and his father had some silly falling-out. With the misguided passion of youth, Elliott never forgave him, and then…it was too late."

"Is that Grandfather's description? A silly falling-out? Because my father didn't hold grudges over silly falling-outs. He was a loving and forgiving man. Whatever happened to him was serious, and it was Grandfather's fault."

Grandmother managed an inch more rigidity in her bearing. "You will not speak of your grandfather like that in his house. Whatever happened between him and Elliott was their business, not yours, not mine. Now, if that's all you want…"

Gazing at her, Reece realized the old woman meant what she'd said. Maybe she'd actually believed it all along, or maybe Grandfather had told her that so often over the years that she'd come to accept it as fact. But the *falling-out* had cost *her* a relationship with her son and granddaughter, as well. How could that not be her business? How could she have not wanted to know why?

"No," she said abruptly as Grandmother began to rise. "That's not all. The summer I lived here…you told me Valerie had left to take care of things back home. Was that true? Or was she receiving treatment for her drinking?"

Grandmother's mouth pursed as if she'd sucked a lime. "You have a habit of asking the wrong people your questions, Clarice."

"Well, Daddy and Grandfather are dead, and Valerie doesn't discuss the past. Since you're the one who told me the lie…"

She soured even more. "Yes. Your mother had to enter a rehabilitative program. I insisted. She was a weak woman. Between the medicines the doctor gave her and the alcohol she took from Arthur's study, she was barely able to get out of bed. But she begged me not to tell you, so I didn't. I had no idea that keeping a promise to her would offend you all these years later."

"I thought she had abandoned me, like Daddy. I thought she'd left me with people who obviously didn't want me any more than she did."

"Your father didn't abandon you, Clarice. He died." Grandmother didn't bother to dispute the last part of Reece's statement, sending an ache through some small part of her that still wanted... Instead, shaking her head, she scowled. "I'd hoped you would outgrow this melodramatic bent, but you obviously haven't. These things happened years ago. Why are you making a fuss about it now?"

Reece wanted to give in to that melodramatic bent and stamp her feet, throw a few priceless antiques and scream, *I was a child! A mourning, distraught, terrified child! I needed love and reassurance and to believe someone wanted me!*

But her grandmother's response would likely be one she'd given before: *You always were rather spoiled.*

"I'm making a fuss now," Reece said, imitating Grandmother's stony calm, "because I can't remember most of that summer, because something happened then, something besides my father dying and my mother leaving me. Something that gives me nightmares, that—" She paused, considering the wisdom of going on, then did it, anyway. "Something that Grandfather's spirit wants to keep secret. He's been warning me away since I got here."

"Oh, really, Clarice." Grandmother put more scorn in those three words than Reece would have believed possible. She rose from the sofa, looking inches taller

and way too imposing. "His spirit…for heaven's sake.
I blame your father for this, encouraging you to believe
in ghosts, and both your parents for this self-centered,
inappropriate and hysterical behavior. Your grandfather
wanted nothing to do with you in life, and he certainly
wouldn't change that in death. As if such a thing were
even possible." At the doorway, she turned back. "I do
believe you should consider ending your visit here soon.
Welcomes do wear out, you know. Sooner for some than
others."

# Chapter 10

"It's human blood."

Jones was standing in the shed door, Maricci beside him, watching silently as the lab geek who'd come with the detective performed her test. Marnie Robinson wasn't much of a living-people person, Maricci had told him, but she was very good with dead people and all things pertaining to them.

Now, at the certainty in her voice, Jones's gut tightened. He'd known it was blood. Reece had been positive of it. But hearing it confirmed made it that much more real.

It *could* be Glen's blood. He could be one step closer to knowing what had happened to his brother.

"Is it as much as it looks?" Maricci asked.

Marnie gazed at him owlishly. "Losing this much blood would be incompatible with living."

"Can you get DNA from it?"

"Depends on the degree of degradation. Can I take the tarp back to the lab?"

Maricci shifted his gaze to Jones, who walked a few yards off to the east, where the building hid them from any view inside the house. Maricci followed. "If we take it without permission from Miss Willa or a warrant, the results will be inadmissible in court, and if there's any way it implicates her husband, she's not likely to give permission. There's a missing-persons case open on your brother. The sheriff's investigator has probable cause to get a warrant."

"The old man is dead. Kind of limits any legal action that can be taken against him."

"If he's the killer."

Everything pointed to Arthur, and Reece was certain it was him warning her away. "Who else would it be? Miss Willa? Mark? Reece? An old woman or a couple of scrawny kids?" Glen had been too wiry, too strong, too used to fighting with bigger and smaller brothers. No way he could have been overpowered by any of those three, unless they'd bashed his skull from behind, and no way any of them could have crept up and caught him unaware.

"I've heard stories about Arthur Howard," Maricci said. "That he was scary, menacing, more than a little odd. I don't have trouble believing he could lose his temper and kill someone."

"You're a detective," Marnie said from the doorway of the shed. "You don't have trouble believing anyone could do anything. Do I bag the tarp or not?"

Both of them looked at Jones. He and Reece had been led to the shed for just that discovery, but not to prosecute a dead man. Not to destroy Miss Willa's life—and besmirching her respected family name would do that—or any chance Reece might have a relationship with her only grandmother. All *he* wanted was answers: Was it Glen's blood? Had he died here at Fair Winds? And maybe, if God took pity on Jones, where was his body?

Maricci turned to Marnie. "Bag it. And get a DNA sample from him for comparison."

Surprise flickered across the woman's face, but she nodded and disappeared back into the shed.

In a few minutes, they were driving away, the tarp and Jones's DNA sample both bagged and tagged. He closed the door, wincing at the metallic shriek, then started toward the house. The tarp's discovery didn't change the fact that he had a lot of work to do.

He was mixing concrete in a wheelbarrow with a hoe when Reece came out the front door. The instant he saw her, some of the tension left his shoulders and jaw, and a smile came automatically. She wore the same clothes as the afternoon before, with smears of dirt, sweat and mortar on both shirt and shorts.

"I didn't bring any real work clothes with me," she commented as she approached, "so I'm already stinky and dirty."

And beautiful.

"How did it go with the detective?"

"It is human blood, and taking the tarp without a warrant means anything they find is inadmissible in court."

She made an obnoxious sound. "Like that matters in this case."

"How did it go with Miss Willa?"

"She confirmed that Valerie was in rehab those months. She also said I was hysterical, melodramatic and unwanted when I was here then, and that I had worn out my welcome now and should consider leaving. Of course, being a proper Howard, she won't throw me out. Not just yet, at least."

Jones stared at her, then took her hand, but she wouldn't let him tug her around the wheelbarrow so he could hold her. Her eyes bright with tears, her fingers holding tightly to his, she forced a smile. "It's nice to know where one stands, isn't it?"

So much for preserving some kind of relationship between them, he thought bitterly. "You don't need her."

"I know." She shrugged. "I never really had her in my life. Just the possibility that someday… But it's okay." She sounded as if she meant it. There was disappointment in her voice, but acceptance, too. Not resignation—that would have been painful for both of them—but simple acceptance.

"Families suck sometimes, don't they?"

She laughed. "Yeah, they do. That's why God gives us the chance to make or pick our own."

They finished the last course of bricks on the south bed, then moved to the bed north of the steps. The sun was warm, the air smelling of the river and the pines that edged the yard but lacking the crisp scent of fall Jones had become accustomed to on many of his jobs farther north. Sometimes he missed the change of seasons, but not enough to move someplace where the months brought drastic weather.

In fact, he might be willing to consider relocating farther south instead, where the biggest seasonal difference was warm versus hot, damp versus suffocatingly damp.

New Orleans would do nicely.

If he had the proper incentive.

Around eleven, Miss Willa drove past in the big old

Caddy, never glancing in their direction. Jones watched Reece's expression, but saw nothing more than momentary curiosity. Soon after, the housekeeper brought out a tray of chicken-salad sandwiches along with two dainty dishes of salad and a pitcher of iced tea. "I fixed the food before Ma'am told me about her appointment with Robbie Calloway," she announced, "and she won't eat leftovers, so I'm not letting it go to waste."

Reece didn't say anything, so Jones thanked the woman. After she returned inside, they gave their hands a cursory wash with the hose, then sat on the porch steps, the tray between them.

"Robbie Calloway is her lawyer," Reece said before picking up a sandwich half. "Either you're getting your contract at last, or I'm getting officially disinherited, if I wasn't already."

"I don't know if I still want the contract." He wasn't sure he'd ever actually wanted the project. His work had been a way to gain access to Fair Winds, to find answers about Glen. If that tarp provided at least some of those answers, and he had this knot in his gut that said it would, would he want to stay around for months on end, working for the widow of his brother's murderer?

Even if he didn't get answers, his opinion of Miss Willa had taken a serious hit today. He wanted to pursue this thing with Reece. How much trouble would it cause if he was working for the grandmother who'd deliberately caused her such needless pain to restore the place that gave her such nightmares?

"Maybe someone who works for you could oversee it," Reece remarked. Then she shook her head. "Strike that. Grandmother isn't the sort to settle for the number-two guy. She'd want your attention twenty-four hours a day until the job was done to her satisfaction."

"Yeah. Some of my clients think a contract with my company entitles them to that." He grinned. "I charge them a little extra for attitude."

She finished her sandwich, then picked up the delicate crystal plate and heavy silver fork, both elaborately monogrammed with an *H*. "I don't see the point of salads like this," she remarked. "A small serving of mixed greens, one slice of cucumber, two cherry tomatoes and raspberry vinaigrette. I like plain old lettuce, and I want lots of stuff on it, all topped with rich, thick blue-cheese dressing. You know, a salad of substance."

"The difference between you and Miss Willa. She's superficial. You're about substance."

"Thank you," she said with a wry smile. "Right now I'm about embracing the differences. It's hard to imagine that my dad came from these people."

"Because he made a conscious decision to leave here. To leave them."

"Like you did with your family."

It was the perfect opening to tell her about his family, both good and bad. He'd rehearsed different openings in his head, ways to tell her his background without making his family seem nearly as bad as hers, because they weren't, honest to God. But the opening came and went without a single word making it from his mouth before she returned to the subject of the contract.

"What happens if you decide you don't want a project? You've got a lot of time in here—these beds, the research, the sketches, all the preliminary work. You just write that off and move on?"

He grinned. "I don't know. I've never turned down a job of this size and significance."

She gazed into the distance a long time, then abruptly

said, "I think you should do it. You and Grandmother both said the gardens here were historically significant. Even if you don't need it on your résumé, who could turn down the chance to bring history back to life?"

"And to thwart Arthur in the process?"

Her smile was sunny. "Well, yeah, there's that, too."

"Pursuing it could bring disaster into Miss Willa's life. Gl—whoever's blood is on that tarp might not have been your grandfather's only victim. Once we start digging out here—" His words broke off as ice rushed through his veins, appropriately chilling to the image of mounds of dirt and piles of bones.

As she looked across the expanse of yard, her gaze darkened. Imagining how many bodies could be buried there? Wondering if her grandfather could have been that kind of monster?

After a moment, her hand unsteady, she gestured toward the two new beds. "At least we haven't uncovered any bodies so far."

He met her weak smile with his own, choosing not to point out that so far, the digging had been relatively shallow. If Arthur were burying a body permanently, surely he'd dug deeper than two feet, as the heavy equipment would. "It would shake Miss Willa's world to its foundations, having to face the truth about her husband."

"That's on Grandfather, not you. If he really did kill someone—maybe multiple someones—those families have the right to know. The world has a right to know what he was." Sounding less certain, she added, "Grandmother would deal with it. She's a Howard. Besides, I could be wrong. That could be Grandfather's blood, or Mark's, from an injury they suffered while out hunting or working."

Jones didn't repeat Marnie Robinson's comment about the blood loss being incompatible with life.

"It was August," Reece remarked.

His gaze jerked toward hers. "What?"

"The day I surprised Grandfather in the garage. It was August. And the truck was in the garage, not the shed."

Glen had disappeared in August. What were the odds that someone else had disappeared from the area at the same time and not been missed?

Not good.

Leaning his head against the pillar, Jones closed his eyes, easily calling his brother's image to mind. Dark-haired and dark-eyed, Glen had usually been smiling, often laughing, always feeling whatever he felt with passion. Jones had wanted a different life, but it had been Glen who first suggested actually trying for it. He and Siobhan were in love, but they'd both been promised to someone else since they were kids. They'd decided on the runaway plan, and Jones had jumped at the chance to join in.

If they had changed their minds, if Jones had warned their parents, if *anything* had happened differently...

*Things happen as they're meant to.* Granny's voice echoed in his head.

Opening his eyes, he looked at Reece. "Do you believe in fate?"

She wasn't quick to answer. She finished her tea, then stood and walked to the bottom of the steps before facing him again. "I do most of the time, but sometimes I wonder. Was it fate that Daddy died so young? That Valerie wasn't the best mother? That I wound up here that summer?" She shrugged, an easy, graceful movement. "I do believe things happen for a reason, that good comes out of bad, but I also believe we have influence, too. We can make decisions that can alter our fate. Though then, Martine asks, how do you know you weren't fated to make that decision?" She smiled faintly.

"What good came out of your father's death, your mother's deficiencies and your summer here?"

Again she smiled, but this time it was the real thing, the kind that involved her entire face and affected him like a punch to the gut. "I met you." She turned, tossing a look back at him over her shoulder, as she sashayed— no other word fit that sassy, sexy sway of her hips—to the work site.

Warmth spread through him, easing doubts and guilts and fears in its path, and for the first time in a very long time, he realized, he was falling for a woman. It was too hard and too fast, at least if a man wasn't prepared for it.

But his subconscious had been preparing for it even if his conscious mind hadn't. All that talk about long-distance relationships, all that wanting—needing—to take care of her, all that thought about relocating to New Orleans... Oh, yeah. Some part of him had been headed this way without his even realizing it.

It was a realization he was very comfortable with.

With the brick border finished on the second bed, they returned to the first one, using spades and rakes to work amendments into the soil. By the time they were ready to plant, the wind had come up and the northwest sky had turned dark. Thunder reverberated slowly across the ground, a low, threatening rumble.

"Great," Jones muttered. If they went ahead and planted before the storm broke and it was a hard rain, it could damage the new plants. If they didn't plant and get the mulch down, the rain would pound the soft soil into mud, complete with rivers and gullies. At least there would be no loss if they didn't plant, just more work for them when the ground dried out.

With the wind whipping into a frenzy, they put away the tools, then, as the first rain fell, took cover on the broad porch. Reece stomped the dirt from her shoe soles on the top step. "Watching thunderstorms was the only thing I liked doing here. A couple times, when we were here, Daddy and I snuggled up in that chair—" she pointed to a wicker rocker "—and we'd count the seconds between the thunder and lightning. Once he told me the scientific reasons for storms, but usually he'd have some silly story about giants bowling or lightning bugs getting refills of light so we could chase them at night."

Jones sat down in the chair she'd indicated and held out his hand. She didn't hesitate at all, but curled immediately, trustingly, in his lap.

Trustingly. When she didn't know some of the most important things about him.

He held her loosely, his hands resting on her hip, and quietly said, "I was here that summer, Reece."

Reece's brows drew together, and her stomach muscles clenched. Surely she'd misunderstood. If he'd been at Fair Winds fifteen years ago, why would he wait until now to say so? Why would he listen to all her angst over not remembering without telling her?

Why would she have trusted him?

His arms tightened around her, and he said, "Wait, Reece, hear me out," before she realized she'd made an effort to stand. She pushed at his hands and he let go, leaving her free to move away, and immediately she felt the loss of his embrace, his warmth, the sense of security he'd always given her.

*Security?* From a liar?

Folding her arms across her middle, she stalked to the nearest column, then faced him. "You forgot to mention that until now?" Her tone was snide, sarcastic, reminding her of both Grandmother and Mark. Maybe she really was a Howard, after all.

"When we met, I didn't know if you just didn't remember me, if Glen and I weren't important enough to have registered with you or if you knew who I was and were pretending not to. I thought it would be better if I waited until I did know to say anything."

"I told you Tuesday night that I didn't remember," she said heatedly, then chilled just as quickly. "You didn't believe me."

He pushed out of the chair with enough force to set it rocking and paced to the end of the porch. "I wasn't sure. I wanted...I needed to be sure."

Borne on the force of the wind, rain splattered her back, but she didn't move deeper into the porch's cover. "What do you mean, you were here? You weren't staying at the house. Grandmother would have mentioned— Mark would have mentioned it."

"I never saw your grandmother back then, and Mark had good reason to keep his mouth shut."

She waited, but when he didn't go on, she flung both arms out. "What reason?"

It was obvious in every line of his body, in his eyes, in the rigid set of his jaw, that he didn't want to answer, but he would. If she had to strangle the truth from him, she would, by God. She even took a step toward him, but stopped when he spoke.

"Your fear of water. Mark tried to drown you that summer. Glen and I stopped him."

It was an outrageous claim. Mark had been a spoiled brat, and there'd been no love lost between them, but *drown* her? He'd picked on her, pestered her, tormented her, but he hadn't hated her that much.

Had he?

Because…it didn't *feel* outrageous.

"In the creek," Jones went on. "Where it forms a pool. You and Glen were meeting to swim, and I was with him, and we saw him holding you under, saw you fighting him. We…jumped in. Stopped Mark. Got you out."

Slowly her arms lowered to her sides. It felt—it felt like truth. As if everything inside her remembered it even if her brain didn't.

Mark had tried to kill her. Yeah, that would explain the memory loss, the determination to never return to Fair Winds again, cutting off contact with her father's family. He'd tried to kill her, and her grandmother, with her talk of melodrama, never would have believed it—if Reece had even bothered to tell her—and her grandfather… He'd probably given Mark tips on how to succeed the next time.

Numbly she went to the chair Jones had vacated and sank down with a creak of wicker. Just a few minutes ago, she'd felt safe in this chair, just as she had all those years ago with Daddy. Now…

She raised her dull gaze to Jones's. "Who is Glen?"

Anguish crossed his face, then disappeared. "My brother. He and I were camping out there near the cemetery. We ran into you one day on our way to the river. You were hurt and scared and so sad, and he always

liked fixing things—machines, animals, people—so…
he was your friend."

"Where is he now?"

The stark emotion flashed again. Her hand lifted, her
fingers reaching out to comfort him, but there was too
much distance between them, and she couldn't bring
herself to close it.

"I think he's dead," he said in a monotone that hinted
at how deep that thought hurt him. "I think that blood
on the tarp we found is his."

Dead. Murdered. Right here at Fair Winds. By her
grandfather.

*Dear God.*

She pressed her hand to her mouth, as if that could
stop the sickening thoughts, but words spilled out, anyway. "You think—you're here—you think we might
find his body. That's why you're here. That's why—"
Helplessly, she waved a trembling hand at the lawn.

He continued in that flat, hard voice. "A few weeks
ago, Glen's belongings were found hidden back there
in the woods, just off Howard property. I left without
him that summer. I figured he was out there somewhere
living his life, just like me, until I heard that news. I
came here hoping to find something, to learn something. When your grandmother asked me to redo the
gardens, it was too convenient. I couldn't refuse."

Of course not. It gave him a reason to hang around
and ask questions. And she just happened to choose the
same time to come back herself. What lousy luck. *Or,*
whispered Martine's voice in her head, *was it fate?*

"You could have told me," she said, accusation heavy
in her tone.

"Not at first. I didn't know what you might say to
your grandmother. I didn't trust you."

Reece smiled grimly as the rain poured harder. She was the one famous for trust issues; she feared betrayal and abandonment and disillusionment, and yet he hadn't trusted her. Ironic.

"So you didn't trust me at first. Do you now?"

"Would I have spent last night with you if I hadn't?"

Some pettiness inside her wanted to retort that she didn't know since he was so obviously good at keeping secrets, but she knew better. Last night hadn't been just sex. They'd both had their share of casual sex, and they both knew the difference.

"So why didn't you tell me sooner? Once you decided I was trustworthy, why didn't you say something?"

He crouched in front of her chair, the column at his back. "I tried last night. But you said, 'Make me forget everything else in the world but you and me.' And I wanted that, too, so..."

*That sounds like the start to more serious conversation, and I can't do it anymore tonight.* She'd meant the words with all her heart. If he'd insisted, if he'd told her any of this then, she would have had a meltdown right there on his sofa, and even he might not have been able to put her back together.

His gaze was steady, intense. Though he was trying not to show too much emotion, it was there in his eyes: sorrow, anger, regret, concern—and that concern was for her. *He's a good guy,* Evie had told her. *In spite of everything.*

Something else Evie had said flashed into her mind. *Do you remember him?* Had Evie known in her woo-woo way that Jones was connected to her past? Probably.

She didn't remember him. But he and his brother

would have been the only friendly people in her life fifteen years ago. Maybe that knowledge somewhere deep inside her explained why she'd so quickly come to feel comfortable with him. To trust him.

"So this thing between us…"

A little of the tension around his mouth eased. "Would have happened no matter where or when we met again."

"*If* we met again."

He shook his head. "When."

She was considering the possibility that everything in their lives had happened in order to bring them together, that they were meant to be. That when Daddy had said he and Valerie were meant to be, it hadn't just been a romantic notion but a fact of life. Even for someone who believed in fate—most of the time—it was an enormous idea to take in.

"I wasn't honest with you from the start, Reece, but I like you a whole lot." His mouth quirked. "I think I'm falling in love with you. Whatever happens here, I still want to see you. Be with you. Be a part of your life."

Honesty forced her to admit that she wanted to be with him, too. She wanted at least a fair chance to have a normal relationship with a good guy—with *this* good guy. She wanted to see if she was falling in love with him, too. All her emotions suggested so, but she'd never trusted any man enough to risk her heart, so it was a totally new experience for her.

And she did trust Jones. Even though he'd misled her.

She gazed past him to the flower bed, where the rain flooded out crevices and puddled and washed away much of the work they'd done, then slowly brought her gaze back to him. "I've always had an interest in gardening."

She saw by his expression that he understood the reference to his earlier words: *Ideally, I'd want a wife who shared my interest in the business.* Tension drained from him, and he rocked forward onto his knees. "I've always had an interest in New Orleans."

"You would visit me there?"

His hand closed around hers, and he eased to his feet, drawing her with him as he stood, holding her close. "Honey, I'd relocate there. I'm no fool. I don't want a long-distance relationship. Always saying good-bye, sleeping alone, waiting to see you again? It might have worked for my parents and grandparents, but not for me."

She wrapped her arms tightly around his neck and felt...peace. Welcome. As if she'd come home.

## Chapter 11

Jones was still holding her, his cheek pressed against her hair, his eyes closed, his gut taut with gratitude, when the air around them crackled. The hairs on his neck stood on end an instant before lightning struck the nearest live oak alongside the driveway. The sound was deafening, the scent crisp. He looked up in time to see a massive branch explode from the tree and across the road, leaving a charred, ragged wound on the ancient trunk.

Still in the circle of his arms, Reece twisted to face the tree, her nose wrinkling at the smell of ozone. "Wow."

"That tree's taken its hits." He let go long enough to point out an old scar a few feet from the new one. "It lost a big branch there, too, at some time."

"When I was here." She said the words casually, but the instant they registered with her, her body stiffened and her next words came slowly, hesitantly. "Right after I came. It was the first thunderstorm since I'd arrived, in the middle of the night. The lightning strike woke me. The windows in my room were open, and that smell... I didn't know what it was. I didn't know what had happened."

Jones could imagine her, already unhappy in this place, getting jerked from sleep by a violent storm and with no one to turn to—no father to hold her and tell her silly stories, no mother to comfort her, no caring grandmother to tuck her back into bed.

"I got up to close the windows, and then I stood at the front window and watched. The lightning was constant, lighting up the entire sky, so bright sometimes that it made my eyes hurt, and the thunder went on and on until it felt like it was inside me. I was about to get back in bed and pull the covers over my head when I saw..."

She was silent so long. His mouth close to her ear, he quietly prompted her. "What did you see, Reece?"

She eased away from him and walked to the first step. "Grandfather. It was pouring rain, and he was carrying something over his shoulder, something heavy wrapped up. He carried the—the—it over into the yard—" she pointed west of the second flower bed "—and laid it down and picked up a shovel and began covering it."

Stopping beside her, Jones watched her hand tremble in the air before wrapping his fingers around hers. Her skin was clammy, the shivers so strong that they vibrated through his own hand. Slowly he lowered their hands, but she didn't seem to notice. She was staring fifteen years distant into the rain, her cheeks pale, her voice losing strength, reminding him of the girl she'd been then.

"I watched until he was finished. He took the shovel and disappeared around the house again. I was always too curious, Valerie said. I wanted to know what was so important that he'd had to bury it in the middle of the night in a terrible storm. So the next morning, I went out front to look. Before he'd dug the—the hole, he'd cut the grass out in big squares, then pieced it back together. Grandmother wouldn't have noticed. I wouldn't have if I hadn't been looking for it."

He could see the scene easily: the bright, sharp-edged light that followed a cleansing storm, the air as damp as the ground, the sad little girl with the pixie haircut sneaking out of the house, curious but totally clueless about the aftershock of what she was about to do.

"I got a stick that had blown off in the storm, and I was crouched there, poking this stick into the ground, when Grandfather caught me. He lifted me off the ground and said, 'If you ever tell anyone…'"

Anger roiled through Jones at the old man for terrifying his granddaughter. Relief that the body she'd watched him bury couldn't have been Glen's, since it occurred before they'd arrived at Fair Winds. Revulsion that Arthur Howard must have killed more than once. Concern about how Reece would bear this.

"The next time I came outside again after that, the first thing I did after making sure Grandfather was gone was stand at the bottom of these steps and pace off the distance to the—the grave. Twelve steps out and twenty-six to the right. I was terrified of him and angry with him and one day I was going to find out what he'd buried and show everyone."

She looked at him, her eyes glittery with uncried tears and a faint, unhappy smile on her lips. "That's why I count."

The rain still fell, easier now, but the lightning had passed and the thunder was nothing more than an occasional rumble. He'd worked in the rain before, for far less important reasons.

For a long time they stared at each other, and finally she nodded. "You get the shovel. I'll count. I'm good at it."

He retrieved a shovel and gloves from the tools covered with a tarp near the drive. When he returned, she'd already taken the first twelve steps and was walking north. "How tall were you when you were thirteen?"

She held up one finger, took a dozen more steps, then stopped. "I don't remember, but I was the tallest kid in my class." Opening her arms, she faced the house. "This is thirty-eight steps for me now. Do you want to allow for shorter legs?"

"Just a little." He sank the shovel into the dirt a few feet closer to the house. It went easily through the first couple waterlogged inches, then required more effort.

How deep did a monster dig when he was burying a body in his own front yard? At least two feet. More than three?

Soaked within minutes, he dug a decent-size hole to three feet. A years-old skeleton didn't make much of a target, so after a few more scoops, he moved again at an angle to the house and started over. He'd stopped to sluice his hair back from his face when Reece asked, "What if it wasn't a body? What if there's nothing left of whatever it was to find?"

"What else would he bury in the middle of the night in a storm?" He muscled the shovel into the dirt, tossed out a scoop of mud sitting atop dry dirt, then stomped it in one more time.

It hit something solid.

His jaw clenched, his fingers knotted on the handle, he loosened the dirt in the area, dropped to his knees and shoved his hand into the hole. About two feet down, he found the object, long and cylindrical, worked it free of the loosened soil, then brought it out.

He recoiled, dropping it to the ground, then swiping his muddy glove on his jeans. Reece didn't show such dismay, instead kneeling in front of him and gently picking it up. "It's a bone. Too short for a leg." She held it alongside her own arm, several inches shorter, and studied it before looking at him. "An arm?"

One nod. That was all he could manage.

"We should call—" Sliding his gloves off, he patted his pocket where he normally kept his cell, but of course it wasn't there. He'd left it on the charger in the cottage, where he'd left Mick, too, asleep on the couch. Reece didn't have hers, either. Her wet clothes were plastered to her body, making that obvious.

"You shouldn't have disturbed the dead."

The voice came from behind them, the tone as friendly as if he'd simply commented on the weather. Reece's fingers clenched tightly on the bone as Jones stood, then turned. The Jaguar was parked in the driveway, just short of the fallen limb, and Mark was striding toward them.

He was dressed down for the middle of a business day, in khaki trousers and a polo shirt, looking as if he'd come from the golf course instead of the office. The elegant-casual look contrasted sharply with the length of pipe he held in his left hand and the small pistol in his right.

"Haven't you heard the old saying 'Let sleeping dogs lie'?" he asked, as polite as any well-bred Southern gentleman could be.

"That's not a dog," Jones replied.

"No, it is not. How about this one: 'Curiosity killed the cat'?" He smiled at Reece and added, *"Meow."*

*Cat, meet Curiosity.*

Looking very unkittenish, still holding tightly to the bone, Reece moved to stand beside Jones. "You knew about this body?"

"Of course. I knew about that one." He pointed where they'd found the grave. "I knew about that one." This time his finger shifted three feet away. "And that one. And that one and that one. I know about all of them."

Jones's stomach heaved. "How many are there?"

"I never bothered to count them. Besides, the number changes. After today, there will be two more."

"Grandmother will be back any moment," Reece bluffed.

"No, she won't. She had lunch with Macy and me at the country club after her meeting with Robbie Calloway. Macy convinced her to attend the historical-society meeting with her. They won't be done for several more hours. Do you know why she went to see Robbie?"

"To cut me out of her will?"

"You were already out of it. Grandfather took care of that when you refused to attend her birthday party." He grimaced with fake sympathy, then scowled. "She put you back in. Can you believe it? She said it was only fair, you being Elliott's daughter, even if you were a ridiculous little drama queen."

"And what? If I die before she does, the money goes back to you?"

"Me and my children."

Reece scoffed. "You can have it. I don't want anything from the Howard family. I don't even want their name anymore."

Though he rested the pipe on the ground, Mark's aim with the pistol remained steady. "I'm supposed to believe that? That you'd turn your back on a fortune because you don't like the people who had it first? I'm not stupid, Clarice. Besides, that's not the only reason you have to die. You're nosy. You always have been. You never learned to respect other people's boundaries. Snooping in the yard, in the garage, spying on Grandfather and me. You want to call the police about that bone, don't you? Let them come out here and dig up the entire property and tarnish Grandfather's name and traumatize poor Grandmother. I can't let that happen."

He moved a few steps closer, and all trace of pleasantness disappeared beneath a cold, angry, insane smile. "I *won't* let that happen."

Reece's knees were unsteady, her lungs tight. She'd accepted that her grandfather was a murderer, but her cousin, too? What the hell was the Howard motto? *The family that kills together...?*

Oh, God, this couldn't be real. None of it. She wasn't standing here in the rain holding all that was left of some poor stranger's arm while her childhood tormentor pointed a gun at her and Jones. Mark had outgrown that behavior; he was an adult, a husband, a father, a likable, respectable man. He couldn't really intend to kill them, could he?

The gun drew her gaze like a magnet. Yes, apparently he could.

"Then your objection to the garden restoration was never about the money," Jones said quietly.

"It was always about the money. But it was also about protecting my family."

"She's your family."

"No, she's not," Mark said.

"I'm not," she insisted. She'd always known the family was a bunch of snobbish, entitled elitists, but now she knew they were also all crazy. She had some personal issues, but insanity wasn't one of them.

She looked at Jones, utterly motionless in the light rain, and thought she'd be damned if she'd let a crazy man kill her when she'd just found the man who could help her deal with those issues.

"So...what?" she asked. "You plan to shoot us and add us to your boneyard? You think no one will notice? No one will wonder?"

Mark shrugged. "Grandmother told you to leave. You left. And when he—" he jerked his head toward Jones "—realized he wasn't getting the contract for the garden project, he left, too. What happened to you after you drove out that gate is anyone's guess."

"That's pretty lame."

"We're Howards. No one would ever suspect us of wrongdoing." He gestured with the pistol. "Let's take a walk."

Reece's feet actually started moving, but Jones didn't budge. "Let's not."

Mark's expression was comical for a moment, then he waggled the pistol. "Man with a gun here. The way this works is I tell you what to do, and you do it."

"That only works if you're undecided about killing us. But you've already made the decision, and you expect us to cooperate? To make it easier for you?" Jones shrugged, looking far less scared than Reece felt. "Dead is dead, whether it's here or in the woods. I vote for here."

What was he thinking? That maybe the housekeeper would come out and Mark would have qualms about killing *her?* That Grandmother would return home early? Or maybe that Detective Maricci would come back with information or new questions? Any of those seemed about as likely as another bolt of lightning coming out of the dreary gray sky and striking Mark dead where he stood.

Furtively Reece glanced around. The nearest cover was the corner of the house, too far to reach before Mark shot them, and the only possible weapons were the shovel a few yards away and the bone in her hands. She couldn't imagine Mark coming close enough for the shovel to be of any use or that the bone would do much, if any, harm before it broke.

If Jones was looking for a way out, too, it didn't show. He looked as calm as Mark, as if this was just any old discussion on a fall afternoon. "You're wrong that no one would suspect you. You know Tommy Maricci?"

"The cop? Of course."

"You remember that tarp out in the shed with the old man's pickup? The one with the big, dark stain?"

Mark's brow wrinkled. "I didn't realize Grandfather kept that truck. He hadn't driven it for years. We had some good times in that truck."

"Yeah, well, Detective Maricci has that tarp. They've already identified the blood as human."

Mark started shaking his head halfway through

Jones's statement. "Grandmother would never let a police officer take anything from this property."

"You're right, she wouldn't. So Reece and I gave it to him. It may not be admissible in court, but all these remains will be."

Two details struck Reece at the same time: Mark's confidence was shaken by that news, and Jones was edging away from her, moving so slowly that she hadn't even noticed. Her first impulse was to follow him, to stay right at his side because she always felt safer there, but she forced herself to not only stay, but to shift just the tiniest bit away.

"You had no right." That cold, imperious Howard tone came through in Mark's voice, making him sound eerily like Grandfather.

Another shrug. "One of these bodies is my brother's. That gives me every right."

Sorrow washed over Reece. She'd forgotten about Glen for a moment. She wished she remembered his face, his friendship, his saving her life, but there was just that big blank. But Jones remembered. He would never forget.

"Where is Glen?" she asked softly.

"Somewhere out there." Mark indicated the expanse of lawn. "We only kept track of graves to know where to dig the next one. But you'll be seeing him soon."

*We only kept track of graves to know where to dig the next one.* God, he sounded so normal, so sane, as if murder was simply a hobby he'd shared with Grandfather, the way other boys fished with their grandfathers, keeping track of which lures brought better catches.

Reece edged another half inch to the right. "Why did Grandfather kill him?"

"He didn't. I did. He didn't respect boundaries, either. He interfered with my plans—snooping around, trespassing, probably stealing anything that wasn't nailed down. That's what gypsies do, you know."

Her stomach tightened and heaved. Mark had been fourteen years old when Glen died, barely into his midteens, and he'd murdered a boy. How could she not have known he was so cold, so damaged?

Because she'd been thirteen. The idea of one kid killing another had been totally foreign to her. Though now she knew rationally it happened, it still felt foreign.

She pushed the ugly thought from her mind, focusing instead on his last comment, stealing a glance at Jones. Gypsies? That was the family tradition he'd run away from? He'd wanted to live a life without the scams and cons and prejudices that were his heritage?

"'Gypsies' is a word the uninformed use," Jones said blankly. "We were Irish Travelers."

Mark shrugged impatiently. "You say Irish Travelers. Everyone else says lying, thieving bastards."

The shovel was within Jones's reach. One quick lunge...and then what? Charge Mark and hope the element of surprise kept her cousin from shooting him? Reece had no idea. All she did know was that she needed to keep Mark's attention on her. Outwardly bold, inwardly quivering, she began walking toward him. The pistol in his hand swung around, aimed straight at her.

"You killed Glen because he stopped you from killing me."

"Yeah. And because I could. He was so arrogant. He stayed to look out for you. He thought he could protect you from me." Mark snorted. "He never even knew what hit him. One instant he was there, hiding behind that tree—" he jerked his head toward the oak that had suffered the lightning strike "—and the next…lights out."

After a thoughtful moment, Mark gestured. "I don't have all afternoon to chat. I'm going to count to three—" he thumbed back the hammer on the weapon "—and if you aren't headed toward the woods, I'll kill you here. One."

Reece swallowed hard. Her feet wanted to obey, but Jones was right. If he was determined to kill them, the last thing they should do was cooperate. Damned if she'd die easily for him.

"Two."

Her mouth was dry, her palms damp. The arm bone she held visibly shook.

Mark's index finger began to tighten on the trigger. "Thr—"

In an instant, an icy wind swirled around them, giving voice to an inhuman roar as dark and menacing as the vortex surrounding them. Reece staggered from the force of the gale, stumbling, and would have fallen to the ground if Jones hadn't grabbed her, supported her. Their wet clothes whipped around them, her hair standing practically on end. Dust swirled in the air, stinging her skin, making it difficult to see, to breathe.

Jones tried to move; she felt his muscles straining, and she tried to herself, but the wind held them in place, rushing with fury, pelting them with rage. With one hand cupped around her eyes, Reece saw the terror on Mark's face as the pipe was snatched from his hand and sent soaring across the yard. He spun in a circle, cursing, searching, then stiffened, his eyes widened, his nose wrinkling. She did the same, smelling dirt, damp and cigar smoke.

"Holy God," Jones whispered.

A figure was taking form at the core of the fierce wind that shook her to her very core: large, threatening, the center of her nightmares for fifteen years. It hovered, shaking so violently that its outlines blurred, and a long, drawn-out rumble vibrated the air. *Nooo mooore!*

Helpless against the spirit's force, Mark managed to squeak out one pleading word. "Gr-grandfather?"

*I told you no more!*

"But—but, Grandfather—" Mark's protest broke off with a shriek as his gaze shifted to his hand. Slowly, moved by an invisible force, his hand twisted, the barrel of the gun pivoting toward him. His elbow jerked out, as a wooden doll's might under the control of an angry puppeteer, and the gun pulled upward.

His expression turned panicked. "Grandfather, no! I was just doing what you taught me! I was just protecting you! No, you can't—"

The gunshot echoed as Jones pushed Reece's face against his chest.

As quickly as it had come, the storm dissipated and the air cleared. Unnatural quiet settled around them, heavy enough to make Reece's ears ring, then slowly she became aware of the rapid tenor of her breathing, the thud of her heart, the slow control of Jones's breaths.

She didn't want to look. Didn't want to see Mark lying lifeless on the ground. She wasn't sure she *could* look. It took all her strength to stay on her feet, clinging to Jones as if she would never let go.

His body was solid, his arms strong around her. "It's okay," he whispered. "It's okay, sweetheart."

Gradually her trembling eased, and she lifted her head just enough to meet his gaze. "Grandfather…"

He nodded.

"He saved our lives." The man who'd terrorized her in life had protected her in death, and he'd done it by... "Mark was his favorite. They were so much alike. And he killed him."

Jones glanced past her, his expression grim, then nodded again. "He wanted the killing to stop."

*I told you no more.* And when Mark had ignored him, Grandfather had taken matters into his own hands. Oh, God, what would this do to Grandmother and the rest of Mark's family? He had a mother, a wife, a daughter, another one on the way. They would be devastated. Grandmother, at least, would blame her, and probably the others would, too.

Not that it mattered. The important people—she and Jones—knew she wasn't guilty.

With a deep breath, she turned in Jones's arms to face her cousin for the last time. He lay on his back, his head turned to the side, his eyes closed. The entry wound was small, the exit, if there was one, not visible from her vantage point. Nothing about him screamed *He's dead!* He didn't appear particularly peaceful, or as if he'd just lived through the last moments of his own terrifying murder. He just looked like Mark.

Mark the pest, the bully, the tormentor. The murderer.

And this yard was his and Grandfather's burying ground.

Her fingers tightened on Jones's arm. "I'm so sorry about Glen."

Emotion shuddered through him. "I knew when I came here he was dead. I felt it. At least now we *know*."

She understood the difference between knowing and

*knowing.* She'd known something bad had happened that summer. Now she *knew* exactly what.

Would it make a difference to him—that his brother had died because of her? Would it change the way he felt about her? She was trying to find the courage to ask when he sighed heavily, his arms tightening.

"Fate," he murmured. "Everything happens for a reason."

Her father's death, Jones's and Glen's desire for new lives, that horrible summer, her return at the same time as Jones's, Mark's secrets, Grandfather finally, for the first time, doing something to protect his granddaughter.

Fate.

She breathed deeply of rain-washed air, the damp of the river, the scents of sweat and soap and Jones and herself, then gently pulled from his embrace. "We'd better call Detective Maricci."

Hand in hand, they skirted Mark's body, circled around the house and headed to the cottage. As soon as the authorities arrived, she figured, the entire property would be declared a crime scene and she and Jones would have to leave. He might return here someday to work, but she never would. The past was over, and Fair Winds had no place in her future.

Even if it had brought her Jones.

She loved fate.

And she was pretty sure she loved *him.*

It had been a week since their discovery of the first body. The excavation had been slow going, but so far, more than forty bodies had been found buried in the front lawn. The authorities assumed the victims were mostly hitchhikers, runaways and homeless people—

the kind of people who could go missing without anyone noticing. They estimated the older graves at forty to fifty years old. Arthur Howard had started his hobby young, about the time he destroyed the gardens.

The thought repulsed Jones: What kind of man preferred moldering bodies in his yard over color, fragrance and well-maintained flower beds?

Glen's body hadn't been identified yet. DNA and dental matches could take a while with so many victims.

*So many victims.* Thank God he and Reece hadn't become two more in the Howards' lifelong killing spree.

Mark's funeral had been private, and Miss Willa had sent a message that Reece wasn't welcome. After the service, she and Mark's family had left Copper Lake for Raleigh, where his mother lived. No one knew whether she would return to the home that had meant so much to her or if the revelations would keep her away. Jones was betting she would be back.

But he wouldn't. There were too many other things he wanted to do. Get on with his work. Live his life. Spend every moment possible with Reece.

They were standing in the nearly deserted parking lot of the motel where he and Mick had first stayed in town. She lifted her suitcase into the SUV, then turned to catch him watching her. The smile that spread across her entire face warmed him from the inside out. She was beautiful. She was everything he could ever want in a woman. She was his fate.

"Are you ready?" she asked, reaching through the open pickup window to scratch between Mick's ears.

"I am." In less than forty-eight hours, they would be in New Orleans, where he would meet her friends, whose approval he wanted, and her dogs, whose approval he needed. He trusted his obvious love for her would be all Evie and Martine would have to know, and dogs always liked him. If Bubba, Louie and Eddie were a little hesitant, he could count on Mick—and plenty of treats—to smooth the way.

He kissed her, and the hunger that was always right there simmering beneath the surface flared. Reluctantly he stepped away, opened the door for her and waited until she was buckled in before he closed it again. After climbing into the truck, he leaned forward to see past Mick's wagging tail. "Hey, you said last week that you didn't want the Howard name anymore. You want to consider mine?"

For a moment, she gazed at him, expression blank. They'd done a lot in the past week: dealt with the cops, made love, discussed their pasts, their present, their future. He'd said *I love you,* and she'd said it, too, but neither of them had gotten around to bringing up marriage.

Then came that sweet, warm smile that danced along his spine and made him want to lose himself with her, and she responded with words he knew he'd hear from her again. "I do."

He grinned foolishly as she shifted into Reverse and backed in a big U around the truck, until they were facing each other again with only a few feet of pavement between them. "Tell me again…is Jones your first name or last?"

Without waiting for an answer, she blew him a kiss and drove away. He laughed as he shifted into gear to follow her. "Settle in, Mick. We're going home."

\* \* \* \* \*

# SUSPENSE

Heartstopping stories of intrigue and mystery—
where true love always triumphs.

**Harlequin** ROMANTIC
*SUSPENSE*

## COMING NEXT MONTH
### AVAILABLE DECEMBER 27, 2011

**#1687 TOOL BELT DEFENDER**
*Lawmen of Black Rock*
**Carla Cassidy**

**#1688 SPECIAL AGENT'S PERFECT COVER**
*Perfect, Wyoming*
**Marie Ferrarella**

**#1689 SOLDIER'S RESCUE MISSION**
*H.O.T. Watch*
**Cindy Dees**

**#1690 THE HEARTBREAK SHERIFF**
*Small-Town Scandals*
**Elle Kennedy**

# REQUEST YOUR FREE BOOKS!
## 2 FREE NOVELS PLUS 2 FREE GIFTS!

## ROMANTIC
### SUSPENSE

**Sparked by Danger, Fueled by Passion.**

**YES!** Please send me 2 FREE Harlequin® Romantic Suspense novels and my 2 FREE gifts (gifts are worth about $10). After receiving them, if I don't wish to receive any more books, I can return the shipping statement marked "cancel." If I don't cancel, I will receive 4 brand-new novels every month and be billed just $4.49 per book in the U.S. or $5.24 per book in Canada. That's a saving of at least 14% off the cover price! It's quite a bargain! Shipping and handling is just 50¢ per book in the U.S. and 75¢ per book in Canada.* I understand that accepting the 2 free books and gifts places me under no obligation to buy anything. I can always return a shipment and cancel at any time. Even if I never buy another book, the two free books and gifts are mine to keep forever.

240/340 HDN FEFR

| | |
|---|---|
| Name | (PLEASE PRINT) |
| Address | Apt. # |
| City | State/Prov. | Zip/Postal Code |

Signature (if under 18, a parent or guardian must sign)

### Mail to the **Reader Service:**
**IN U.S.A.:** P.O. Box 1867, Buffalo, NY 14240-1867
**IN CANADA:** P.O. Box 609, Fort Erie, Ontario L2A 5X3

Not valid for current subscribers to Harlequin Romantic Suspense books.

**Want to try two free books from another line?**
**Call 1-800-873-8635 or visit www.ReaderService.com.**

* Terms and prices subject to change without notice. Prices do not include applicable taxes. Sales tax applicable in N.Y. Canadian residents will be charged applicable taxes. Offer not valid in Quebec. This offer is limited to one order per household. All orders subject to credit approval. Credit or debit balances in a customer's account(s) may be offset by any other outstanding balance owed by or to the customer. Please allow 4 to 6 weeks for delivery. Offer available while quantities last.

**Your Privacy**—The Reader Service is committed to protecting your privacy. Our Privacy Policy is available online at www.ReaderService.com or upon request from the Reader Service.

We make a portion of our mailing list available to reputable third parties that offer products we believe may interest you. If you prefer that we not exchange your name with third parties, or if you wish to clarify or modify your communication preferences, please visit us at www.ReaderService.com/consumerschoice or write to us at Reader Service Preference Service, P.O. Box 9062, Buffalo, NY 14269. Include your complete name and address.

HRS11B

*Brittany Grayson survived a horrible ordeal at the hands of a serial killer known as The Professional... who's after her now?*

*Harlequin® Romantic Suspense presents a new installment in Carla Cassidy's reader-favorite miniseries,*
LAWMEN OF BLACK ROCK.

*Enjoy a sneak peek of*
*TOOL BELT DEFENDER.*

*Available January 2012*
*from Harlequin® Romantic Suspense.*

"**B**rittany?" His voice was deep and pleasant and made her realize she'd been staring at him openmouthed through the screen door.

"Yes, I'm Brittany and you must be..." Her mind suddenly went blank.

"Alex. Alex Crawford, Chad's friend. You called him about a deck?"

As she unlocked the screen, she realized she wasn't quite ready yet to allow a stranger inside, especially a male stranger.

"Yes, I did. It's nice to meet you, Alex. Let's walk around back and I'll show you what I have in mind," she said. She frowned as she realized there was no car in her driveway. "Did you walk here?" she asked.

His eyes were a warm blue that stood out against his tanned face and was complemented by his slightly shaggy dark hair. "I live three doors up." He pointed up the street to the Walker home that had been on the market for a while.

"How long have you lived there?"

"I moved in about six weeks ago," he replied as they

HRSEXP0112

walked around the side of the house.

That explained why she didn't know the Walkers had moved out and Mr. Hard Body had moved in. Six weeks ago she'd still been living at her brother Benjamin's house trying to heal from the trauma she'd lived through.

As they reached the backyard she motioned toward the broken brick patio just outside the back door. "What I'd like is a wooden deck big enough to hold a barbecue pit and an umbrella table and, of course, lots of people."

He nodded and pulled a tape measure from his tool belt. "An outdoor entertainment area," he said.

"Exactly," she replied and watched as he began to walk the site. The last thing Brittany had wanted to think about over the past eight months of her life was men. But looking at Alex Crawford definitely gave her a slight flutter of pure feminine pleasure.

*Will Brittany be able to heal in the arms of Alex, her hotter-than-sin handyman…or will a second psychopath silence her forever? Find out in*
**TOOL BELT DEFENDER**
*Available January 2012*
*from Harlequin® Romantic Suspense*
*wherever books are sold.*

USA TODAY bestselling author

# Penny Jordan

### brings you her newest romance

# PASSION
# AND THE PRINCE

Prince Marco di Lucchesi can't hide his proud
disdain for fiery English rose Lily Wrightington—
or his attraction to her! While touring the palazzos
of northern Italy, the atmosphere heats up…until
shadows from Lily's past come out….

*Can Marco keep his passion under wraps
enough to protect her, or will it unleash itself, too?*

### Find out in January 2012!